DEATH ON THE FRONTIER

DEATH ON THE FRONTIER

by

PETER E. S. KING

Stethoscope Publishing

105/2 Clarke St, Crows Nest, NSW 2065 Australia

First published in 2025 by Stethoscope Publishing

Text © Peter E. S. King
Cover artworks by Ted Lewis
Design by BKA+D

Typeset in Adobe Garamont Pro

Printed and bound by Ingram Spark

978-1-7638987-3-8 (paperback)
978-1-7638987-4-5 (eBook)

Death on the Frontier, King, Peter E. S.

A catalogue record for this book is available from the National Library of Australia

To Old Friends

Graham Norman Crouch
Inspector of Police at Cowra
1989 – 1993

And

Lenny Grahame
Policeman at Gooloogong
1990-1996

THIS IS BOOK THREE OF A SERIES

CAST OF CHARACTERS

HILL TOP

Norman Green – *Police Sergeant*

Ian Percy – *Mounted Policeman*

Bill Todd – *Mounted Policeman*

James Wade – *Mounted Policeman*

John Hale – *Mounted Policeman*

Willie Darkwood – *Mounted Policeman*

Rex Howard – *Mounted Policeman*

Barry Hodge - *Policeman*

Charlie Wickham – *Storekeeper*

Ma Shell – *Runs Food Tent*

Ned Doncaster – *Grog Shop Owner*

CITY POLICE

Jimmy Straw – *Police Inspector*

John Sefton – *Police Inspector*

Alex Pitt – *City Constable*

Charley Rush – *City Constable*

Ben Holt – *City Constable*

Jamie Tyson – *City Mounted Policeman*

HADE FAMILY

Sam Hade – *Ex-Army Doctor and Squatter*

Elizabeth Hade – *his Wife and Nurse*

Andrew Hade – *Eldest Son*

Patrick, Shaun and Toby – *Younger Sons*

Jenny Hade – *Daughter*

HUNT FAMILY

Alex Hunt – *School Teacher – Sunny Flat*

Joan Hunt – *His Wife and Innkeeper*

Betsy Hunt – *Daughter and Cook at Inn*

Bob Pringle – *Ex-Police and married to Betsy*

Tom Hunt – *Carrier*

Dick Hunt – *Carrier*

Jason Hunt – *Shop Owner at Sunny Flat*

GILL FAMILY

Alan Gill – *Squatter*

Eva Gill – *His Wife*

Victor Gill – *His Son*

Anne and Betty Gill – *Twin Daughters*

SUNNY FLAT

Greg Knoll – *Police Sergeant*

Eddy Redwood - *Blacksmith*

OTHER POLICE

Roy Cook – *Policeman*

Steve Baker – *Undercover Policeman*

Ken Taylor – *Undercover Policeman*

Jason Stone – *Undercover Policeman*

Sergeant Rich - *Murdered*

Frank Black – *Corrupt Policeman*

William Knox – *Corrupt Policeman*

Fred Noll – *Works for William Knox*

Albert Cross – *Works for William Knox*

Andrew Willow – *Green Hill Policeman*

Nick Rose – *Mounted Policeman*

Harry White – *Mounted Policeman*

SQUATTERS

Red Bryant – *Squatter*

Mary Bryant – *His Wife*

William Carter

Stuart Cameron

Tony Bolt – *Son of Squatter*

Allan Waters – *Son of Squatter*

Susie Seaway – *Adopted Mother of Steve and Roy*

Margaret Straw – *Wife of Jimmy and sister of John Sefton*

Richard Stafford – *Cousin of Margaret Straw*

Harriet Hodge – *Wife of Barry Hodge*

Julian Webb – *Harriet's Brother - Squatter*

The Old Man – *Kabaicha - Spiritman*

Old Herman – *Storekeeper in Deep Glen*

Jack Lessing – *Security Guard*

Abe Kane – *Security Guard*

Bertie Howard – *Younger Brother of Rex*

Alec Brick - *Stockman*

Chapter 1

The settlement of Hill Top had been established because of its position between two gold fields now abandoned. The police had built a small slab building in place of the original tents. With the growth of the community this had been extended as the numbers of mounted police needed to patrol a large area grew. It was now a substantial slab construction with room for nine men, with a Sergeant's office on the northern end of the building. At the other end, and separate to the main building, was a partly open slab shed for cooking and an eating area.

The community was a combination of tents of various sizes and quality, and slab buildings anywhere from good too dangerous with a muddy track between them in winter and a dusty one in summer. On the edge of the dwellings were open cesspits which were not pleasant in the hot months, some were filled in and others freshly dug. As with all bush communities they were situated close to water, as buckets had to be carried each day.

Sergeant Norm Green was in charge of the police barracks and at times had to endure the visit of an Inspector, who felt it his duty to come and check that all was in order in this part of his District. Most of these Senior officers were aware that Sergeant Green had an extraordinary knowledge not only of his patrol area but of other places too. He was always treated with respect, if not a little envy at his local knowledge, which had been made possible by family members living in these harsh areas. Many had married men who craved to own land and became pioneers in developing a good living through hard work on the land they loved, forever moving forward into isolated areas whenever the opportunities arose.

These men and their families were only too pleased to welcome the police out on patrol, for a mug of tea or a meal and of course all the distant news. In many instances these visits were their only connection to the outside world, except for the travelling Priest or Pastor and later a travelling salesman who also carried news. In these remote areas men were seeking wealth any way possible either finding gold or stealing it. Keeping it was a lot harder as men had to be paid for their silence.

The Sergeant very rarely revealed what was in his mind, this intelligent network was second to none and no other sergeant wanted to take his place at Hill Top, perhaps when it was no longer on the frontier, the job would have an appeal for a quiet life. Perhaps his knowledge of men was his greatest asset and this was exhibited in the quality of the men who worked with him. There were now nine mounted men who operated out of the station. He gave them "out of uniform" time and were well known in the community, not always as respectable men! They enjoyed the grog shops and that particular establishment at the lower end of the row of tents on the edge of the settlement. As with most communities where churches had been planted, there was tension between certain establishments, respectability was the desired normal and rarely achieved in remote communities. Men worked hard and played hard, where there were few women in the tents or huts.

Sergeant Green was a fine man for fielding the complaints made frequently by Mr. Charlie Wickham, who made a habit of complaining almost every time his police had been relaxing in the community. It was well known that Mrs. Wickham was behind all of these visits. She had had an unfortunate experience eighteen months ago, when she was walking on the arm of her husband, past the opening of the tent of the 'night ladies'. A visiting drunk policeman had said to Charley that he ought to choose a younger girl and not the old one on his arm! The policeman was required to leave Hill Top before sunrise the next morning. The community rocked with laughter for the next week. As the middle-aged Sergeant sat at his desk, he refused to think of himself as old and thought about his men. He could chuckle about their various escapades behind a closed door but showed a different face when they stood before him at his desk.

In front of him was a letter from Inspector Jimmy Straw, whom he had known from past jobs which had extended into his area of the frontier. The letter informed him that the head of the undercover branch of the police was missing and requested information about where Inspector John Sefton might be, as it was believed he was somewhere in the area. He had been investigating a certain problem, exactly what wasn't revealed in the letter. Only two undercover policemen were being sent out to investigate any known sightings of him. Both men were known to him, Alex Pitt and Charley Rush, and considering how long the letter had taken to get to him, he thought they might arrive this morning.

Down at the stables Willie Darkwood, a fair-haired young policeman with a good physique and cheerful personality, walked out of the doorway to see two horsemen ride into the yard and dismount. He recognised Alex Pitt but wasn't too sure about the other man.

"Hello Alex, is that a prisoner you've got with you?"

Alex answered his greeting with a wide grin and the other man expressed himself in clearer terms.

"Willie me lad, any more f— lip from you and I'll know what to do about it!"

Willie grinned entirely unrepentant and said, "I wasn't sure Charley, I don't know where you got those old clothes, but I'd give them back!"

"We're undercover Willie."

"It certainly smells like it from here Charley!"

"It's meant to, you bad excuse for a policeman!"

There was laughter from a couple of other men waiting to select their horses. As soon as the horses were unsaddled and put out in the paddock, Alex and Charley walked up to the Sergeant's office, one whiff of Charley and the usually unperturbed Sergeant suggested, "Let us continue our talk outside under the tree."

Alex cheerfully agreed as Charley explained, "I've been amongst the great unwashed.

"Have you not crossed any creeks on your way to Hill Top?" The Sergeant enquired.

Alex pretended not to be listening as Charley replied, "Not enough water in them to drown a mouse, Sergeant."

Alex coughed.…..The Sergeant had thought he had heard every excuse under the sun and realised he was mistaken. For a few moments he gazed at Charley and then said with the smallest twitch of his lips, "Quite so."

They settled down to talk about the missing head of the undercover department of police.

"How long have you both worked for Inspector Sefton?" The Sergeant asked.

"Since the murder of Sergeant Rich."

"I don't understand, why are you here now he's missing?"

"We received a note from Inspector Sefton to get out of that side of the mountains as quickly as possible. He indicated our lives were in danger. We were instructed to ride to Hill Top."

"Do I understand you are Sefton's men?"

"Yes Sergeant."

"Do you know other men in this barracks?"

"Yes Sergeant, most of your men we know as friends or at least as workmates."

"I will require you both to think carefully and tell me as much as you can remember, over the last couple of months about life in his office or elsewhere, particularly in the time after you returned from the closed valley operation."

"We talked about it on the way up here. He went missing a couple of weeks before Steve Baker and Roy Cook turned up at his office, they arrived twice wanting to see him," Charley mused.

"William Knox was angry and tried to make them leave. Inspector Straw agreed to see them, which later we were told by Knox, because they already knew Ken and Steve had saved the life of his son, Dommy in the closed valley," Alex added.

"He gave them new information about their family, but one of Knox's men was listening," Charley continued.

"That office has ears and eyes in the walls to every room, nothing is secret and it has become dangerous with two camps," Alex explained.

"There was a storm of protest when the men discovered the Counterfeit Reward money was used to acquire those three blocks of land for Steve, Roy and Ken. For some reason not yet explained this act by Sefton caused his disappearance," Charley said quietly.

Both the Sergeant and Alex looked surprised and Charley laughed at their expressions and explained, "Whoever takes any notice of a pile of old clothes in the corner of a room."

There was stunned silence as the Sergeant made a discovery, along with Alex about a man they thought they had known quite well - he was a natural gifted listener. For all his humour and the shield he wrapped around himself in company, he was a dangerous man with this ability.

The Sergeant smiled at Charley and thought aloud, "I'm glad you're on our side in the coming difficult times."

The men laughed and Alex asked, "What can we do in this situation?"

"Stay a few days and get to know all of our men and then ride out to find any information regarding John Sefton or in particular the people who wish him harm."

As they began to walk away he called out to Charley, "No upsetting Charley Wickham or his wife again, please Mr. Rush."

He smiled as Charley mumbled something in reply…

Chapter 2

The best tent for good quality food in Hill Top was Ma Shell's tent. No one was ever brave enough to ask what lay beneath the surface of the simmering pot on the fire, at was almost black but tasted wonderful, if you were hungry. Most of her customers came back time after time, as her food filled empty spaces and was cheap only a penny or two. Ma was a rough old woman, with a questionable past, but kindly with a sense of humour to match her other qualities. She really loved handsome young men and they always received a cheerful welcome, none more so than the young policemen, knowing a good deal about them from her friends in the lower tent. Charley, who had a well-deserved reputation as a good cook, though with a slim figure, decided to go along with Ian Percy, Willie Darkwood and James Wade, who chose Ma's soup over the food being offered at the barracks that night as she was good company in a tent full of men.

Ma greeted James and Willie whom she had come to know quite well, in particular as they happily met equally her ribald humour, which caused laughter throughout the tent. They gave as good as they got but never unkindly, and in this manner were well received by her regular customers. Charley ate slowly and gave every indication that he enjoyed the meal, even having a second helping and, in the process, winning Ma's heart as she gave him a big hug and told him he could come anytime to her tent. Charley grinned and left words in his mouth unsaid.

"It isn't like you to be silent Charley," Ian commented on the way out of the tent.

"No, she's a good woman and a f— good cook, we don't share secrets and I'd love to know what herbs she uses in that pot."

"This your first visit?"

"Yes, to her tent.'

"Now what about the grog shop?" James suggested.

Yes, but not the one under the tree, it nearly killed me a year ago." Charley responded.

"You were warned I seem to remember Charley," Ian replied and laughed.

Charley gripped Ian's arm above his elbow and explained, "At that time we didn't know what a bush patrol was going to be like, nothing we'd ever experienced would equal it, as you well knew at the time. The grog was the worst I've ever tasted, riding and emptying one's guts wasn't good."

"This grog is about the best you will find out here," Willie said to Charley.

They entered a large tent with logs as seats and slabs of wood across stumps pretending to be tables, which weren't flat and mugs were forever falling over, and of course they had to buy another one, to the delight of the owner.

James and Willie settled down to a mug of ale which tasted a lot better than expected. They were told it was fresh which meant it had been recently made out back of the tent, perhaps even watered down to go further and would anyone know the difference as the night progressed. No one noticed as James didn't follow his colleagues, except Willie who whispered, "Don't get caught."

"I won't, keep them occupied."

He went to the lethal grog shop by the tree and bought a mug of spirits and returned to his colleagues. Waiting for an opportunity he switched mugs beside Charlie Wickham. The storekeeper was accustomed to drinking his ale in one mouthful which pleased his companions who owned other tents or slab buildings in Hill Top and dealt with the local people. These men weren't popular and recently Charlie Wickham had been complaining again about the off-duty young police. The eyes which had seen young James switch the mugs nudged their neighbours and slowly there was an expectant hush in the otherwise rowdy room. They watched like a cat with a mouse, as Charlie raised his mug expecting soft ale and instead got firewater, the whole lot went down his throat. He had trouble breathing, tears streamed down his cheeks and at last he gasped out, "I'll have the bastard who did this whipped and run out of this community."

There were peals of laughter from the delighted men with cries for more ale. Charlie looked around and saw the police and demanded in a loud voice, "I command you to arrest someone."

"Who would you like me to arrest Mr. Wickham?" Ian asked in a mild tone.

"Whoever changed my mug."

"Accidents happen on grog counters, it obviously wasn't meant for you, so why did you drink it?"

"It was where my mug is usually placed."

"Mr. Wickham, I suggest in future you be more careful what you pour down your throat in a public place."

"Let's go, a whole lot of people need a good whipping," Mr. Wickham grumbled to his friends.

Glaring at the police as he passed them and noticing Ian's eyes, he refrained from saying another word. Earlier Ian had seen the humour exhibited by James and Willie, and he was reasonably sure which one was the culprit.

"Anyone for the lower tent?" he asked as they were leaving.

Charley declined saying, "Not after a long day in the saddle, I'm for the bed."

The young men followed Ian down between the tents towards the last one.

"Ma said there was a new girl who hasn't been treated with respect and Ma asked us to look out for her, after all she is a working girl," Willie said quietly.

"Happy to oblige." James replied.

Ian, who had heard this conversation, smiled.

The next morning Sergeant Green called the men together to direct the various patrols. Each man received his instructions for the job needed to be done, one of which was out to the Hade farm. His sister, Elizabeth, married Sam Hade and they had four sons, Andrew, Patrick, Shaun and Toby, plus two daughters, Jane and Jenny who everyone believed was engaged to Fred Hall. John was one of their colleagues, he'd met Jenny eighteen months before, when she had nursed him after he'd taken a bullet.

As each of the men left the barracks to do their patrols, the last group were Ian Percy, Bill Todd, John Hale and Willie Darkwood. The Sergeant placed emphasis on his request, "You must be at the farm before the Carriers arrive, the Hunt brothers Tom and Dick. They are to make a delivery of some kind to the Hade family. At the same time one of the men will pass on some information to us. This will be delivered as privately as possible, they carry messages for us secretly, so please be careful."

"If we are asked?" Ian enquired.

"No one is ever to think you are carrying information. You are going out to see Fred Hall who is on leave of absence to get married."

"I was under the impression that John was leaving us for good, due to constant problems with his leg," John said.

"Mr. Hale you are correct, but not just yet, he is to be our man in that area for some time."

They left the office and went to prepare to leave the barracks and walking to the stables.

"What happened to Fred Hall's leg?" Willie asked John.

"The bullet entered the thigh above his knee in an awkward place."

"Couldn't the doctor fix it?"

"Willie, Fred was a long way from that kind of help, though a doctor did attend to him. That's how he got to know Jenny Hade, the doctor was her father."

Within the hour they rode out of the barracks horse yard, travelling west. Being still early spring, they were able to carry meat for the first camp, the second night was after a long day in the saddle. The horses walked at three miles an hour, the State wasn't keen on spending good money on quality horses for the police. A steady mount plodding along at their usual pace, was necessary to survive the long patrols.

Quietly Willie asked John all kinds of questions. He learnt that Bill Todd grew up beside the Nepean River and had worked in a brick kiln, and a shop before joining the police. At the second camp he'd seen Ian dive into the waterhole, which created another question.

"He inherited his colouring from his Great Grandmother, who was a Spanish lady," John explained

Willie learnt that Ian was born and educated in England in a boarding school, and at 16 years old he'd been sent to India and served in the army. Living in India with the climate being hotter than England was the beginning of his habit of washing every day regardless of the weather and he expected his colleagues to do the same. At first Willie wasn't too keen on washing daily, but soon learnt Ian meant exactly what he said about the need to wash.

"Willie you smell like a dead horse, get in the water now or it will be clothes and all. I mean it!"

He complied with a sharp eye on Ian, as he walked into the water up to his neck, before swimming down the pool close to the bank.

"I liked the cold water, I learnt to swim in warmer water," he later he said to John.

"It's better in summer, we can wash our clothes and they dry within an hour," John smiled and said.

Willie soon came to realise that Bill and Ian were night people and John and himself were morning men and talked the whole way through breakfast. The signs were growing but neither John nor Willie took much notice until the end of the second breakfast when Bill had had enough of their cheerfulness.

"Can't you two shut up for three hours or more in the mornings. If you can't be quiet go away, I don't want to hear a fucking sound tomorrow morning," he said coldly.

He stomped away to un-hobble his horse, followed by Ian. John and Willie looked at each other and laughed, while putting out the fire and packing up the camp before following the two grumpy men who hadn't surfaced until after midday and were poor companions for the remainder of the day. The evening meal was eaten in a gloomy silence. As Willie went to his swag he heard Ian and Bill talking quietly as usual at night.

The next morning when Bill woke up, he was looking forward for his first mug of tea of the day, after a wash. As he made his way to the waterhole, he saw in disbelief that there was no fire burning in the camp. He swore under his breath as he searched for the swags of the young police, but there was no sign of them anywhere.

"Where in the fucking hell are you young bastards?" he called out, now properly riled.

There was total silence, as his words faded amongst the trees.

"What's the matter Bill, you're acting out of character making enough noise to wake the dead!" Ian woke up and asked.

"There is no fucking fire burning."

"Wash first," Ian stood up and said

Walking back from the waterhole he smelt smoke and meat cooking. John and Willie were laughing and looked quite relaxed at their fire. Ian had the humour to smile, which turned into a laugh, as he turned and walked back into their camp to find Bill washed and packing away his swag.

"Bill you did tell them to go away, if they wanted to talk at breakfast," he said gently

"I didn't expect them to take me seriously."

"They're just around the corner of the creek, cooking the last of the meat if you're interested in the first meal of the day?"

Bill walking slowly and being watched by his friend, eventually led his horse towards the fire around the corner of the creek, to find it burning on low coals with two slices of meat attached to a stick away from most of the ants, but there was no sign of the young police. Ian looked down the valley and saw two men waiting on the crest of the hill. Eventually Bill and Ian arrived and not a word was spoken for the remainder of the day. Bill and Ian refrained from the strong desire to strangle a pair of young police before sunrise. They in turn talked and laughed quietly, so as not to disturb their aging colleagues. This wasn't to say that sometimes a hand didn't caress a neck or two and to be met with a grin. Knowing they were perfectly safe except in the waterholes, where honour was maintained and scores evened up.

Chapter 3

It had been close to nineteen months since Ian, Bill and John had stayed at the Hade farm, after the gun battle in the valley of the Black Mountain. At that time the family were making clay bricks, to replace the wooden slabs of their house. This work was now completed and a commodious homestead was visible above the flood level of the meandering creek. The house had been built on a small hill and was now surrounded by a wide verandah and a shingle roof. Even from a distance it looked impressive and as they rode closer, there was evidence of fruit trees and a garden adding colour to the previous drab surroundings.

With Bill's knowledge of brickmaking and operating a kiln, he'd spent a day in the clay pit helping the family, after their employees had gone to the gold fields. Ian never wanted to see that pit again, it had been the type of work he had avoided all his life! John had been excused from the pit because he was looking after the two policemen who had been shot, Ben Holt and Fred Hall.

"Didn't you ever play with mud pies when you were a little boy?" Bill had asked Ian.

Bill smiled at this memory, he had received a blank stare and he laughed at the memory. As they rode across the creek, Bill explained his humour and wondered what it would've been like to grow up without the freedom he'd known as a boy. Now riding up to the stables at the back of the house, there was a shout of welcome from Sam Hade, who came out of another hut which had the forge in it, wearing a thick hide apron. His wife Elizabeth came out of the house, followed by her daughters Jane and Jenny. As yet no sign of the four boys. Bill complimented the Hades on the completion of the brick buildings, and they all beamed with pleasure.

"We would've finished sooner if we could've kept you Bill and your men!" Sam said.

"You were fortunate to keep them for one full day in the pit. Wild horses wouldn't pull Ian back into it!!" Bill laughed and replied.

Everyone laughed and no one noticed Ian giving Bill a dig in the ribs or Bill's sudden laugh. Willie had been introduced and made feel welcome and was now sitting at a long table listening to this vibrant family, talking and laughing with Bill, Ian and John. The light from the doorway was suddenly darkened as four young tall handsome men strolled into the room. Willie was amazed at the effect their entrance had on his three colleagues. They were on their feet in seconds and greeted the men warmly. He was surprised to see the three younger men hug John with sheer joy. For almost an hour no one could get a word in between them, as the talking or the laughing never stopped.

"Have you heard how my shadow is doing?" Willie heard Bill ask Andrew, who was the elder of the brothers.

"Tom Thorne is now six going on seven, I see him sometimes, Toby sees him more frequently than anyone else and he's doing well. His sister Betty is now a sixteen-year-old and seems to have got over that unpleasant event. The father Alf Thorne has made a number of improvements to their hut and lifestyle."

"Good to hear, I've wondered about that family."

"Does Charley still eat watercress?" The younger brother, Patrick asked.

Bill laughed as did the younger brothers Toby and Shaun. They told Willie the story gleefully, before asking about Alex and were pleased that all their friends were happy and well.

"When is the big day?" Ian asked Jenny.

She looked at her Mother and Elizabeth replied, "We thought early summer, when Fred is to leave the police."

"Fred is leaving general duties, but he isn't leaving the police," Ian said, smiling gently.

Sam put his hand on the arm of his wife and before she could express her feelings, Sam spoke gently, "I told you Lizzie, Norm Green won't let Fred go just yet, let us hear what is being proposed, before you say things about your brother."

Not to be silenced that easily she spoke forcefully, "My brother needs a good tanning."

"Mrs. Hade, not at his age!" John laughed and said.

She looked at the men who were grinning, took a breath and said to Ian, "Continue please Mr. Percy."

"Sergeant Green is of the opinion that Fred is too good a policeman to let go entirely, so he has made him a Special Constable for this area. He will be required to send reports from time to time about anything happening out here."

"We're happy with that arrangement," Sam said.

His wife had other ideas and expressed, "We're happy today, I don't know about tomorrow."

"Have I heard correctly that you and Fred have created a Partnership to clear the valley of trees?" Bill said to Andrew.

There was a sudden silence and Andrew spoke, "The fat is in the fire now", as his three younger brothers spoke at once.

"What, clear the trees away from where in the valley?"

Three pairs of accusing eyes were staring at him. They were men but the valley had been their playground and they still kept secret paths in the undergrowth, as he had discovered after the fight with the felons and the rescue of Betty Thorne after she'd been raped. Those tracks still existed and as much as he loved his brothers, he wanted to control his land. It would be just like them to do a raid and think it funny when they disappeared and he wouldn't be able to find them.

"You all know I'm planning to clear the valley floor of trees, except those either side of the creek," he sighed and said gently.

"Why Andrew?" Patrick asked.

"I'm going to live in a house up near the waterfall and Fred is planning to build his house down near the end of the valley. We have bought the land on the western side which joins the Hade land. We have also bought the entire valley."

Bill and Ian smiled at each other remembering over a year ago when Fred had talked to them about investing some money he had put aside. It had obviously paid well. Half an hour later Fred Hall walked into the room and before he'd greeted his colleagues, Patrick, Shaun and Toby plied him with questions watched by the Hade family with amusement.

"My soon to be brothers-in-law, if you think for one moment that I will keep all those trees growing close together intact, you have obviously made a huge error of judgement. I know full well that the hill above where I plan to build a house for Jenny, is riddled with your secret tracks. We both know you could raid our vegetable garden and disappear without a trace and think it a great joke," John said cheerfully, when at last they drew breath.

Everyone laughed knowing this is exactly what would happen.

"I will clear enough for protection and you can plague your brother on the eastern side of the valley!" John continued.

"No. Patrick, Shaun and Toby you can help me clear the trees, when Dad has no jobs for you to do." Andrew said firmly.

"Do we have to Dad?" Patrick turned to his father.

"Yes, you know we all help each other. Fred can't marry Jenny until they have a dwelling. We'll have family days working in the valley."

At Bill's request they camped down on the creek near the lovely water hole. They weren't on their own for long before Andrew and Fred came down bringing meat. Later the three younger Hade men arrived with freshly baked damper and wild honey. Willie didn't feel left out at all as they included him in their conversation and humour. Willie spent the next two days in their company assisting them in their daily jobs or just being useful in whatever they were doing. On the second day they took him to the valley in Black Mountain. He was impressed with the secret cave and the stories of the fight. He enjoyed their company and didn't look forward to leaving the farm.

In the weeks and months ahead Willie was to look back at this patrol to the Hade farm as the happiest of the carefree days, before the dark clouds arrived and gradually joy seemed to be fading away as the troubles mounted in their lives. There were no dark clouds over them at this time, that period was still on the other side of the horizon.

Chapter 4

illie was away at Black Mountain when Sam alerted Ian and Bill to the approaching dray now crossing the open plain in front of the homestead.

"You know the company I believe," he said to Bill.

"Yes, Ian and I know Tom and Dick Hunt," adding, "His father Alex was a schoolteacher and taught John Hale at school. He was close to that family in childhood."

"I'm constantly amazed at the truly interesting people we meet on the frontier. I'll have a talk to John before he leaves here," Sam said and smiled, adding in almost a whisper, "The carriers can camp down with you. I'll send meat down for them. You and Mr. Percy can be further down the creek; I'll send Andrew down to make the fire and put meat on it for you."

"Do you have any idea of what we're doing out here on your farm?" Bill enquired.

"Norm hasn't enlightened us, other than he is facing a problem which every policeman dreads above all other difficulties. This carrier has information for you. Regardless we have as usual enjoyed your company and my boys like Willie Darkwood. If it turns really bad you can always send him out to us."

"So you have a fair idea?"

"Yes, Willie is young like my three boys, don't hesitate to send him Mr. Todd."

"I'll keep it in mind Mr. Hade."

"Please look after my brother-in-law, I do realise he's your Sergeant, but he's our family too."

Turning away from Sam, Bill saw the carrier much closer and following the road to the creek crossing. He had a full load with some odd shapes.

"My wife has ordered some material, we would have made some additions sooner or later, but Norm has sent some furniture for us. This simple act on his behalf, tells that whatever else is being carried is of vital importance to Norm. The trust he is placing on you, Mr. Percy and John Hale, I hope isn't misplaced," Sam said.

"You can be absolutely sure we will always stand by our Sergeant."

They left the front verandah and walked around to the back of the house to see a multitude of parcels being unloaded by the two security men employed by Tom Hunt, who were introduced as Abe and Jack. Bill greeted them as he had met them a year or so ago.

"On long trips like this one Tom needs men to protect his dray and its contents, they can keep those who would otherwise attack at a distance, particularly at night," he explained to Mrs. Hade.

While he was speaking to Mrs. Hade, Tom Hunt completed the unloading and John Hale came around the corner of the house and Tom greeted him with almost a hug, to her surprise.

"We were boys together and John used to raid my Mother's little cake tin!" Tom explained.

"Mrs. Hunt is a very good cook and she made the best little cakes, Tom and his brothers encouraged me to raid the tin, because they weren't game to, but they were happy to share the loot of course!!" John grinned.

Tom immediately rejected his interpretation of the earlier events to the amusement of those standing around the dray.

The furniture which Norm had sent comprised of a drop sided table, two comfortable chairs and a wide range of materials, including enough white material to make a wedding dress.

"Mr. Hunt before you go down to your camp come and have a mug of tea with your two men," Mrs. Hade said to Tom.

Abe and Jack thanked her for the invitation and declined as Jack explained, "We've been travelling at a harder rate than usual and a camp is what we need now."

"We understand and will send some meat down in a few minutes."

The men left the stables after attending to their horses and followed Toby down to the usual camp site on the creek.

Sitting around a long table drinking tea Tom Hunt turned to John and said, "My sister and Bob Pringle are engaged and hope to marry in the late spring. Sunny Flat is growing into a larger community."

"Does that mean you will stay at Sunny Flat?"

"Yes John, we're making our home there."

"Bob Pringle is an ex-policeman whose gift is cooking, Tom's sister Betsy is also an excellent cook. They run a food tent.." Bill explained to the Hades.

"No longer a tent, the combined family business made it possible for Mother to open an Inn in Sunny Flat. Our sheds are at the back of it and Dad, as you know, has taken up teaching again and has a large room at the other end of the building. Bob and Betsy have a large eating area at the other end of the Inn," Tom interrupted.

"Are they still drawing a large group of people to their meals?" Bill asked.

"It is always full, the locals have to book a table," Tom laughed and replied

"And your brother Jason?" Bill enquired.

"His shop is now an extension in brick to the Inn."

"If ever we travel down through Sunny Flat, you can be sure we will stop at your Mother's Inn," Mrs. Hade said.

"You'd be made welcome Mrs. Hade," Tom responded.

Sam stood up and said, "I think it's time for you men to get on with your business. Andrew has prepared a fire at the camp site further down the creek, with views in all directions, it's private and he's left a parcel of meat for you."

"My men?" Tom enquired.

"Andrew is with them now and will stay until you return to their camp."

Tom smiled and said

"Thank you Mr. Hade, they are good men, a little rough around the edges, but that is what is needed to stay alive out here."

They all left together and walked down to the creek, collecting quart pots on the way. Tom checked on his own men and received cheerful replies. Leaving this camp they continued walking along the bank and startled a few wild ducks, who took to the air in a flurry of wings. Bill, Ian and John would remember this day and the visit to the Hade farm as one of enjoyment, of laughter and trust in their cheerful company. Even now talking to an old friend in a lovely setting, they wondered what Tom had to say which was so important.

Chapter 5

The meat was cooked and consumed while general conversation was exchanged about their lives. After the tea was made and each mug filled, the men leaned back against the logs in the early evening, the sun low in the western sky.

"Before I give you the information I carry, I need to give you the background to a city problem, which is now in your patrol area. What do you know about Roy Cook's and Steve Baker's background?" Tom said quietly.

"We only know that Steve Baker is a brave man and Roy Cook is his faithful friend," Ian answered.

"My brother Dick and myself have carried messages for John Sefton since we became carriers. We know another family who are in the same business, who have known him for many years. I do know that Steve and Roy are not the children of either the Baker or Cook families. Who their actual father is, we don't know but have a suspicion," Tom explained. He sipped his tea and continued, "When they were young children John Sefton took an interest in them and gave them jobs to do which had rewards attached. These rewards paid for their education, which was more than sixth class. You must remember these boys were little more than street urchins who have seen the very worst of human behaviour and experienced a good deal of it themselves." Tom took another sip of his tea, "These boys proved to be faithful to John Sefton, time and time again which earned his respect. They have also fiercely protective of their adopted Mother who has acted being a prostitute for years but is in fact a gatherer of information. The men who constantly visit her all work for John Sefton."

Tom was clearly not enjoying the need to tell his friends the background to the actual message. He poured himself another mug of tea from his quart pot and continued speaking.

"Their adoptive Mother has vanished, all her belongings from her tiny dwelling in the street has gone."

"Does anyone know where she is at this moment?" Bill asked.

"No. Your job is to tell Steve and Roy."

"There is something else isn't there that you haven't told us," Ian said, eyeing Tom carefully.

"You have always had the ability to see into the heart of a matter, and yes there is something else which is at the core of this entire business," Tom said, smiling at Ian.

He took another sip of tea and explained, "You may know that the boys were given grants of land with the reward money for locating the Counterfeit operation, This was the act which set off this entire problem. It caused jealousy in the department to overflow into murder, and total fury that two street kids were given this reward money in the form of grants of land."

"They aren't street kids any longer, they've proved themselves as men, and good men who are police men, trained in a different way, to do a difficult job and they deserve the land." Ian said thoughtfully.

"Tell that to the faceless man who has let loose the dogs on John Sefton."

"Do you have any idea who is directing the attack?" Bill enquired.

"No, other than he is a policeman."

"He could be anybody," Ian mused almost in a whisper.

"He has police working for him with promises of one kind or another, very likely money," Tom added sadly.

"Who can we trust?" Bill asked.

"Nobody who has arrived at your barracks from the city or anywhere else, until you are sure they are Sefton's men or free of both camps," Tom replied.

"I've experienced this lack of trust in a small community in another country, it is the most destructive emotional blight to invade a group of men. It can destroy friendships and it won't be good in our small barracks," Ian added.

"We're friends with Alex Pitt and Charley Rush," Bill said clearly upset.

"Not now, until you are certain they're working for John Sefton," Tom said equally sad.

"We know they worked in John Sefton's office and have come looking for him," Ian said thoughtfully.

"Ian, Bill, you have to be sure of these two men, if you give them your trust without being certain you may be responsible for John's death and the boys will follow." Tom sighed and as if pushed to the wall added, "Two men, who worked for John and supplied information to a man they thought they could trust, were found soon after in an alley with their throats cut. Beforehand they sent a message as to what they'd done, so a note was passed, we were unable to save their lives."

Ian and Bill were disturbed at what the lack of trust was going to mean among their colleagues and Bill kept saying in a whisper, "I don't like it."

"Ian, Bill you have each other, you have Willie and me. We will manage quite well, there will be problems to overcome, that is part of it," John, who had remained quiet now stated.

"I have a sealed envelope to go to your Sergeant Green, who will carry it?" Tom continued after finishing his tea.

"Ian will take it," John said.

Tom stood up and lent down to pick up his quart-pot and said, "I do wish you well, this is a nasty business. We'll be leaving before sunrise."

They shook hands firmly all round and Tom walked out into the night. John began to put out the fire and pick up his quart-pot, Ian pushed the logs back from the still smoking coals and sat down again saying, "We'll have to tell Willie, what do you think is in the envelope?"

"It's best not to know until we're informed by the Sergeant," John answered. He looked at Bill and said cheerfully, "Cheer up Bill, it isn't good for you to be in a bad mood at night and in the morning or we'll be wanting to get rid of you, if someone will take you!!"

John ducked as the remains of the water in Bill's quart-pot sailed over his head, dancing out of the way he said laughing, "Missed!!"

Bill relaxed enough to say, "What happens now?"

"I'm going to try and not think about it until we return to the barracks. We'll tell Willie at tomorrow night's camp. This is on the way to the job we have to do at the gold field," Ian replied.

Bill keeping an eye out for that tiresome John and what he might be doing said, "I had forgotten about that job, it'll take our minds away from Tom's words for a while anyway."

Back at their camp sleep evaded both men for some time. John slept well, not letting the thought of the lack of trust get to him, that was in the future. When Ian and Bill awoke it was to the sound of John's and Willie's laughter and the scent of meat cooking. It was one of those mornings when Patrick, Shaun and Toby descended on the camp and loudly wondered why certain older men were still in their swags when all the birds were awake!

"They were late getting into their swags, probably like Andrew." Bill heard John explain.

"Andrew is always poor company at breakfast; he loves silence and growls at us. We once brought in a dog which was always growling, thinking they'd be good company. Andrew didn't see it that way." Toby said.

"Andrew would get on well with Bill and Ian then!" John smiled and said.

Bill and Ian endured their company for breakfast as they had brought more meat and told funny stories about their big brother. Some of the stories caused them to laugh and Bill, seeing John's expression, was almost tempted him to throw something at him! The Hade's were a close family.

Chapter 6

Andrew was up in time to have a few words with Ian and Bill as they caught their horses and saddled them near the stables.

"Dad told me last night what you are facing at Hill Top in the near future. Dad meant it when he said, if Willie needs any time away, send him to us."

"Andrew, if we send him to you he may be in a bad state of mind not knowing who to trust."

"Have you forgotten Dad's a doctor and my Mother is a nurse?" Ian responded.

"You win Andrew. Did your enterprising brothers really get a dog to growl beside you at breakfast, so you'd have company?" Ian smiled and spoke.

Andrew laughed at the memory and explained, "They did indeed, the dog growled within about a yard of me and with three pairs of interested eyes watching me, what could I do but growl back at the dog, it shut-up and I had my meal in silence. I never let on that as soon as I could escape their eyes, I laughed."

"What's it like having brothers like the ones you have in your life?"

"I never know what they'll do next, it's one scape after another and always laughter. I often wonder what kind of men they will be, if they ever grow up?'

"I think you're a fortunate man, they love you and their mischievousness is a sign of the closeness of your relationship with your brothers. If they get into a situation which needs a fourth hand, it's to you they'll ask for help, now and when you are older men." Ian said thoughtfully.

"Dad told me you see things clearly in people and around you. He was amazed that the person you call the Old Man made contact with you. Dad says you'd be the only man he'd sat down with at your campfire." Andrew said, staring at Ian.

"He told you about the Old Man?"

"Yes, Dad wanted to tell me about you."

Ian smiled and spoke quietly, "Andrew if ever you meet the Old Man, you will instinctively know beyond any shadow of doubt, that you are in the presence of a great man and you'll treat him with the utmost respect. Anything else and you will never forgive yourself."

"That's what Dad said."

Ian wondered what Mr. Hade had experienced out on the frontier.

As at the previous times the police were sorry to leave the Hade farm and the hardworking family. They rode for most of the day and made camp beside a waterhole. After the meal, Ian explained to Willie what Tom Hunt had passed on to them the previous night.

"We'll need to be aware from now on where we place our trust, to give an example, if we become involved with anything out of the ordinary, we will have to be very careful of the words we use." John told him.

"I couldn't have put it better John, we're entering dangerous territory, so my friends tread carefully," Ian commented.

"Are you saying there are police like us who are crooked?" Willie asked almost in disbelief.

"Yes Willie, they want something owned by other men and are prepared to kill to get it, in the meantime they are attacking those who are supporting the men."

"Willie just be careful," Bill added.

"But who do we know we can trust, if they are police just like us?"

"We don't know Willie, we just don't know," Ian responded.

Willie wasn't dumb, he'd seen all kinds of life growing up, he knew men committed crimes to fulfill dreams, but this was police, men who were paid to protect the community. Bill watching his face as he thought about what Ian had said.

"Willie didn't your father tell you, never stand in front of what another man wants?" Bill asked.

"Yes he did tell me, but we weren't talking about our colleagues."

"This is another aspect of the problem," John said quietly.

"John Sefton and his men are standing firmly in front of their commitments. Other police have another agenda which is the opposite of what is good and correct," Willie said, grasping the idea.

"I couldn't have put it better Willie, that is the problem in its clearest form," Ian smiled.

"Roy and Steve have the land in our patrol district and that's why we will be in their sight. Also I suspect they want to remove anyone who will be able to give evidence after the boys have had the land taken from them," Willie continued quietly.

Bill smiled and before he could say a word, John spoke, "Willie you have grasped our problem and the other difficulty will be who in our barracks is on the other side?'

"I know I can trust you three," he said.

"How can you be sure Willie?" Bill sighed and asked.

"You wouldn't be explaining the problem so clearly if you were on the other side, would you?"

'The seeds of mistrust have been sown and now we will be living with that evil vine growing in our barracks, we have a good group of men working to defeat this evil," Bill mused quietly.

With these words the men retired to their swags and silence reigned except in the tree tops, where birds watched for prey to crawl into their sight.

Chapter 7

The next day they continued to ride north towards the gold field, each man keeping his thoughts to himself. Only Ian knew what was to come in their small community, he wondered how the lack of trust would take shape. There was always something which was the trigger and they'd all know about it.

Bill was the leader on this day as he rode out in front and they crossed relatively flat country in the fresh spring weather. Occasionally they stopped to let their horses graze on the fresh green shoots sprouting from the seeds buried in autumn.

In the mid-afternoon Bill noticed Ian smiling and asked, "What are you so happy about this afternoon?"

"There is a call in the wind, we are going to see an old friend."

Bill almost stopped riding as he twisted on his saddle to look at his friend "Oh! No."

"Don't be like that Bill, it's been over a year since we've seen him, he'll be at our camp tonight," Ian grinned at him.

"Are you sure?"

"Yes, and you'll be a good friend and catch a fish or two and we'll give him damper and some of the wild honey, he'll be quite happy."

"Why do you think he's visiting us?"

"I don't know, I'm just pleased that he is making a visit."

"Who's visiting us to-night?" John asked.

"The Old Man, an exceptional man, who was once a leader on this land, in fact I'd say that while he is alive, nothing has changed. I'm honoured that he comes to our camp," Ian replied.

"Why Ian?" Willie asked.

"Willie, you are about to meet a man you will always remember, how this will be I can't say, each man who sits in front of him comes to his own conclusion."

John looking around from horizon to horizon said, "Ian there isn't a person in sight anywhere, yet I've heard stories, what do you say Bill."

"I try and not think about it where he is concerned, he's outside my world and I'm on his land."

"John look into his eyes and perhaps you will have your thoughts on this matter," Ian suggested.

"Does he have those tribal kings on his back?" Willie asked.

"Yes he does and we don't ask about them, it would be impolite, remember that he's a guest at our camp, and as Bill said we are on his land."

Ian chose a camp site with good running water and a deeper waterhole near it. Bill and Willie walked up the creek to find a place to find a fish or two in the late afternoon. As John prepared the fire and put the quart-pots full of water near the fire, he slowly became aware of an unusual silence, above his head in the trees. He saw empty tree branches and looking round saw no wild animals in sight. A shiver rolled down his spine. This was a foreign land. He thought about what he had been taught in the church at home, which was quite inadequate information when riding over this ancient landscape on horses. Frequently the horse stopped, head thrust up and ears straight up, it saw something and refused to walk in the required direction. Although it was unseen to the rider, the horse made a detour around whatever it didn't like in front of it. This wasn't an empty land at all, it was filled with all kinds of interesting experiences. John thought for a moment of the prayer book he carried in his saddle bag and wisely forgot about it. He was looking forward to meeting a representative of the land itself.

Bill and Willie returned with two fish and the men moved swags, checked the hobbles on the horses, as they would sense the Old Man and might be spooked at the unseen. At last in the early twilight seated around the fire with a place beside Ian, they waited.

Ian became aware and said loudly, "You are welcome at our camp."

An ancient man seemed to appear from beside the old gum tree, he was thin and wore an animal skin, he walked with a stick and smelt of animal fats. The men noticed everything about him, except all these minor details meant nothing compared to the air which surrounded him. So much so that automatically each man stood out of respect, each man in his own way assessed this ancient man in their midst. He was far more than words could convey into their mind.

John wasn't afraid and looked into the Old Man's eyes as they were introduced and the ancient one smiled at him, full of a unique understanding.

'Liquid black eyes of a depth in centuries, beyond calculation," John thought later.

He felt quite humbled at being in the company of such a man even if it was only for a short time. He ate the fish and beamed at the damper and wild honey. Later Ian told him about their problem with the crooked police taking what didn't belong to them.

"Blackman same white man. I fix," the Old Man laughed and said in his broken English, then looking straight at Willie said, "Is why I came. "You brave man, you not tink so, you be happy boys on dark high hill," he continued.

Willie was so surprised he just looked at the Old Man, who suddenly reached across the side of the fire and took his hand quite firmly. Willie, in looking at him, didn't feel threatened in any way at all.

"You mus' 'member. You mus' 'tink an' 'member what you hear. If can't feel me 'ands and see eyes."

As the Old Man was speaking, Willie didn't feel he was at the fire surrounded by friends He felt he was somewhere else, tears trickled down his cheeks, he didn't cry or make a sound as he felt his hand being held firmly.

The Old Man smiled and spoke, "Boy, you brave man, I keep eye on 'oo."

In those few moments time seemed to stand still, Willie could never explain to anyone else let alone to himself why his tears flowed that night. The Old Man was obviously pleased with him and a few minutes later stood up and said with a grin at each of the men, "I go."

He faded into the night and not a sound was heard of his passing. At last in their swags they heard again the chattering of the birds high on the tree branches and were contented their world was back to being normal.

In the morning Willie asked Ian, "What did he mean?"

"Don't be concerned, I heard and understood his words."

"Did he really come to see me?"

"The Old Man doesn't lie, if he said it, it's true."

"How does he know?"

"Willie the Old Man walks in the past and into the future, just accept his knowledge that he came to give a way forward in a time of trial."

All the men spoke quietly among themselves as they rode along about the previous night's visitor, but many thoughts were kept unspoken.

Soon after mid-day Ian announced, "We ought to reach the gold field in the hills opposite us now by mid-afternoon. Bill and I will ride into the camp to make contact with Ned Doncaster, who made the complaint."

John and Willie were only too pleased to make camp beside a creek, a reasonable distance from the miners, as their two companions rode up the creek to where men were panning for gold. The tiny community was doing quite well, having a general store and a grog shop. It was to the grog tent that Ian and Bill rode up to, alighted and tied their horses to a small hitching rail under a tree, and walked into the tent. There were a few logs for seats and a wooden slab across two barrels.

The man behind the counter eyed them for a moment and heaved a sigh before saying carefully, "What'll ya have, I've some good ale?"

"Mr. Doncaster?" Ian asked.

"Who wants to know?"

"We do."

"Police?" Ned said, satisfied.

"We've come at your request," Ian replied.

"F__hell, you actually came!"

"We generally do when problems arise."

"Do you have someone who can look after your business for a couple of hours?" Bill asked.

"Yes I do, what do you want?"

"We want you to tell us exactly what the problem is in this community, then to provide some old clothes for one of our men to go and see for himself."

Ned grinned and talked, explaining in detail. Later he said, "I'll need to see your man and take some measurements and what size he takes in his boots. I'll call the wife and get my horse. Can I give you a cold ale?"

With a mug in hand Ian and Bill liked the ale and thought it must be from Ned's private cask. They finished the ale and went outside to see Ned come riding up between the row of tents. Mounting their horses they led him to their camp. Ned soon had Willie measured and he suggested, "I'll be back within the hour or so with the clothes, they won't be clean, they'll be miners gear."

"Willie won't mind!" Bill said.

"He can go for a swim!" Ian grinned.

Ned commented about the water in the creek saying, "It isn't that warm yet."

"Willie won't mind Ned," Ian said cheerfully.

Ned looked at Willie with a sympathetic expression now having a fair idea that Willie had no choice in the upcoming cold swim. Willie returned a slight softening of his features, knowing Ian would demand a good wash at the end of the job. An hour later Ned returned with a bundle of stinking old clothes and a pair of old boots; if they'd ever seen better days it was before he was born, thought Willie!.

The next morning now attired in dirty old clothes, Willie walked along the creek bank to the mining camp. No one took the slightest notice of him as he walked down the row of tents to the general store. He smiled to himself, he was cleaner than most of the men he saw going down to the creek. He almost laughed aloud thinking of Ian being a miner in filthy clothes!!. He reached the store which wasn't much of a place, just a tent with a wooden lean-to against a tree. It was filled with poor quality mining equipment and he was shocked at the prices. In his hand was a small glass bottle with a cork stopper.

"The owners insist on payment in gold and the scales are crooked according to Ned and there is something else not quite right, which he declined to tell me, so just keep your wits about you." Ian had explained to him after handing him the bottle.

Now as he entered the shop he noticed a sharp faced woman watching him like a hawk, he had a gift of being able to act like a young man not out of his teens. This was how he acted in this shop, it helped that his beard was short like a boy. The woman was summing him up, he could feel her eyes on him or most like he was to be a victim of some kind? He paid in gold for the items on the counter, he saw her in a quick sleight of hand change his gold for a similar one with specks of gold in white sand.

"This boy tried to cheat me with sand," she shrieked loudly.

It was a brilliant performance. Willie was grabbed by her man and marched out of the shop and pushed into the mud and hit by a club for good measure, which hurt. He looked up to see John, Bill, Ian and a good number of the miners. One of the men stepped forward and helped him stand saying, "We all know how it works, we've seen it time and time again."

Ian stepped up to the man and said, "You're both under arrest for cheating the public and stealing gold."

"That kid tried to cheat us, arrest him why don't you?" the woman immediately claimed.

"That man you're calling a kid is a policeman who saw your sleight of hand with the gold," Ian said sternly.

"Tomorrow there will be an auction of this general store, unless anyone wants to buy it outright and deal fairly with the miners?" Bill said loudly.

The man and his woman protested and John said, "You dealt unfairly with the miners and stole their gold, now you will have justice meted out to you."

"There are a couple of men who can take these two criminals to the local court sitting in the next settlement called Scot's Hill. They're escorting two other men to court," Ned suggested.

Ian handed them over to the Special Constables and retrieved his bottle of gold to be returned to Sergeant Green. They left the problem of the stolen gold to the Special Constables to deal with it as they saw fit. A couple of miners combined to buy the contents of the store to continue the business.

The old clothes were returned along with the boots. Willie took to the water like a fish and never showed that it was bloody freezing after a good run once out of the water. The next day they rode back to Hill Top with Tom Hunt's news.

It was a slow ride with Ian and Bill riding together as usual and Willie and John in the rear.

"Trust at the best of times isn't easy because fellows all want something out of life, which others also want," Willie commented, then added, "So what happens?'

"That's the problem Willie, you can't trust a man who wants what you'd like to have in the general run of life."

"Two friends can work together to achieve an end which is satisfactory to both of them," Willie suggested.

"That's the best way and beware of men who aren't your friends," John replied.

Up in the front Bill and Ian talked about Tom's information.

Back at the barracks after unsaddling their horses, John and Willie went up to the meal room, while Ian and Bill went up to the office and knocked on the door. Hearing a word of encouragement they entered to see Sergeant Green leaning back on the only comfortable chair in the room. He indicated with his hand that they were to be seated on the well-worn stumps in front of his desk. Ian gave a full report on what Tom Hunt had told them and put the envelope on his desk. He asked for their opinions and at the conclusion of Bill speaking, said quietly

"You haven't told me anything new about the current situation which has spread into our district. What you have told me, is that the danger is already here. Betrayal operates on money, it will be necessary to quietly discover each man's private life where money plays an important part. We can't do much to protect ourselves in our own barracks, as we have to keep secret those whom we have been asked to protect."

Before leaving the office Ian told him about their encounter with the Old Man. The sergeant asked questions and showed considerable interest in this meeting.

"This is the most interesting news I've been told today. He's well known and greatly feared by his own people," he said. adding after a moments reflection, "All the old Spirit men are treated with a deep respect and kept at a long distance if possible. That he seeks you out and talks at your camp fire is extremely rare."

"Do you mean other white men have seen him?" Bill asked.

"No. He is invisible. When he travels on his business which is judge and jury, his people keep well away from him. They know of his powers. For some reason he wants Willie to do something which he cannot do. That it has something to do with our problem is of interest to us."

Bill and Ian stood up and left the Sergeant to open the letter in private, before they'd walked out the doorway Sergeant Green added, "Have an early night and come and see me in the morning for your next patrol and be ready to leave."

Meanwhile John and Willie had consumed a mug of tea and gone and completed a couple of jobs, replacing items in their saddle bags ready for the next patrol. After sufficient time had elapsed they returned to see if the food was available and saw George Nash sitting at the long table.

"Where have you been Willie?" he asked, looking up from his plate of food.

"Out doing a gold field job"

George shifted on his seat and faced Willie directly saying, "I hear you went to the Hade farm, a bit out of your way I'd have thought."

"Not really."

"What did you go there for?"

"Sergeant Green sent some things out for his sister."

George stared hard at him and asked, "I heard a Carrier was out there too, what was it doing there?"

"Delivering furniture, George."

"Was that all?"

"Yes George, what else would you expect a carrier to be doing at the Hade farm?"

"I don't know, I'm asking you."

John, who had gone to get their plates of food, now returned and put one down in front of Willie. He looked at George and asked, "Why the sudden interest George, you normally never show the slightest interest in our work."

"Just curious."

Ian and Bill had come into the meal room in time to hear the last of this conversation.

"It's begun," Ian said in a whisper.

George completed his meal and left the room after a quick glance at Ian.

The next morning as the sun was rising Bill and Ian were about to knock on the office door, Sergeant Green arrived just as a beam of light touched the top of the hill on the eastern hill. Officially the day had begun.

"I'm glad you're here early, I want you to visit an Inn and grog shop combined in the tiny community of Deep Glen near the ranges. It isn't far from the abandoned gold field, where you found Bob Pringle. Do you remember, it was a bit more than a year ago?" he smiled and said.

"We know it," Ian replied with a grin.

"The envelope had information that John Sefton was at Deep Glen, get whatever knowledge is available please," he continued almost in a whisper.

They left the office, picked up their swags and saddle bags and went to the stables. Soon the horses were caught, saddled and Ian attached his flat leather pouch to just below his quart-pot, this was for frying fish. Bill had acquired some extra rations and was ready as Ian mounted his horse, they rode out of the yard and turned east. At the same time Bill noticed John and Willie riding south on another job. Ian saw his expression and said, "They'll be safe enough."

They had ridden for a couple of hours before Ian said, "The George Nash I've come to know has been a solid man, quiet and not interested in anyone else or their activities. This is the first time I've heard him ask direct questions. More disturbing to my mind, how did he know we'd been to the Hade farm?"

"Perhaps Tom needs to check his security men," Bill suggested.

"Did we see anyone else at the farm?'

"No."

"At the first opportunity I'll send a message to Tom and he won't like it."

The ride out of Hill Top with Ian's words echoing in Bill's mind was quite disturbing.

"What can we do?" he asked.

"Nothing, we'll have to wait and hear from Tom after he gets my message."

"He'll be in their line of fire now, I hope he gets it in time. Ian how far is this problem likely to spread?"

"I don't know. I do know that I wouldn't want to face it on my own. We have John, Willie and the Sergeant, who else?"

"I'd think Alex, Charley and Alf, I'm not sure about the others. I agree I wouldn't want to be facing these faceless men on my own."

Chapter 8

They rode for two and a half days from fairly flat country to the more tightly grouped hills in the east. During the ride they crossed a well-constructed road, maintained by road gangs. It was the main thoroughfare from near the Blue Mountains to a small community beside a river in the inland. It wasn't an easy road for drays and other forms of transport with too many hills. In winter the gullies and creeks were full of water and almost impassable, with many getting bogged.

"The authorities will have to find a better route than this Lachlan road, as the frontier opens up there will be more opportunities for development on the land," Ian commented.

At last they reached the top of a high wooded hill and saw the community of Deep Glen in the valley below. As usual there was water and from a distance, it looked like a small tightly packed community in a small flat valley, with slab and tent dwellings on the high ground. It hadn't taken the pioneers long to discover the difficulty of flash floods, after heavy rain and the necessity to build on high ground, but not too far as water had to be carried in buckets each day. Bill noticed gardens, fruit trees and English bulbs flowering. Pioneers carried their birthplaces with them in the form of what was most familiar to them.

Ian saw as they rode down the hill a slab building with a hitching rail outside it.

"That building could be the grog shop and looks like a general store beside it?" he suggested.

"There's a small slab building behind it," Bill suggested, eying the buildings.

"So there is, now that is unusual."

It was mid-morning as Bill and Ian rode down into the quiet community. There was a dray outside what Ian thought was the general store, but no one paid them much attention as they stopped and alighted at the hitching rail. A man came out of the store with an arm full of parcels and put them in his dray. Seeing the police, he straightened up and said, "G'day."

"Good looking horse you've got in the shafts," Bill replied.

"Yes, she's a prime one."

"Quiet place, what do people do around here?" Bill continued.

"Mostly squatters with sheep and horses," The man replied leaning against his dray.

"Law abiding?" Ian asked.

The man smiled and replied, "Mostly, men lose a sheep sometimes, this road is patrolled by police, away from it you are on your own so to speak."

"In other words normal!" Bill said with a smile.

The man laughed and agreed before climbing up into his driving seat.

"I'd better be going, enjoy your visit to Old Herman," he replied.

Pointing to the doorway. They watched him leave and disappear around the corner of a group of tents. Bill stood aside with a grin on his face beside the doorway, indicating with his hand that Ian enter first, they grinned at each other as Ian entered the store. It was neat and tidy, not in the least like what Ian was accustomed to seeing in these communities. An old man with a well-trimmed white beard stepped forward from a curtained doorway at the back of the room.

"What can I do for you gentlemen?" he asked.

"You have a clean and tidy shop," Ian commented.

"Yes, thank you, I like it that way. We don't get dust storms in this valley and it's easy to keep clean."

Bill enquired

"We've heard that you have experienced an unusual event with two men claiming to be policemen."

"I did, they were bad men," Old Hermon smiled and answered.

"Please tell us what you experienced?" Bill asked.

"If you come next door through that curtain, I can serve you some good ale and we can talk about what happened," Old Herman suggested.

Ian followed Bill though to the grog area, which to his surprise was equally clean with fresh straw on the floor, and noted there wasn't a cob web in sight! There were beautifully made slab seats and a long table down the middle of the room, a most impressive place and Ian commented again on the state of the building.

"My sons work with wood, I learnt the trade in the old country," Old Herman replied.

Both Bill and Ian had been aware that his double u's sounded like vees and made no comment on his obvious origins, they were accustomed to meeting people from all over the world who came seeking gold.

Old Herman began to tell his story. "It was late in the afternoon when a gentleman arrived carrying a bag, he spoke well and anyone could see he'd known better times. He was drinking a mug of ale, when two rough looking men came through the doorway. They said they were police and proceeded to attack the gentleman, who acted surprised. There were a couple of strong men also having an ale, they went to his aid and in the process laid out one of the men, the other backed away."

Old Herman took a mouthful of his own ale and smiled as he continued, "I know police. These men were not police, but they called him a name. Later I wrote it down in case someone came asking questions."

He rummaged in a box of papers and said at last, "Here it is, his name was John Sefton."

"We're interested in him," Ian said.

"Is he a criminal?" Old Hermon asked.

"No. But his life is in danger from bad men."

The old man smiled and explained, "You have justified my actions, The rough men demanded I lock him up in my back shed for the night. They watched me lock the shed, but later when they were asleep, I went out and showed John the unattached wooden slab on the back wall."

"What happened?" Bill asked.

"He moved it and stepped out of his cell. I gave him food and at that time, the carrier Dick Hunt was travelling through Deep Glen and took him away down south to safety."

Ian laughed and getting his breath back spoke, "And the next day?"

"The crooks went and unlocked the door and found the back slab on the ground. They were angry and I thought for some reason they were afraid, it was odd and they refused to pay me, and left soon afterwards, they were bad men."

"Did you record the names they used to each other?" Bill enquired.

"Yes, I did write their names down, but I still remember, Fred and Albert."

"Anything else?" Ian asked.

"Yes, my English is improving. They have not yet met English, I think they grew up down in a cave, a long way down!!"

Ian and Bill stayed for a meal and paid the few pennies required by Old Herman, mounted their horses and rode up the hill in the early afternoon

"That would be Fred Noll and Albert Cross, now working for William Knox and the other faceless men," Bill said.

Back at Hill Top the information was passed to Sergeant Green, who was obviously pleased.

Chapter 9

John and Willie rode out of the police yard at hill Top and turned south.

"Do you think we are under observation?" Willie asked.

"Almost certainly, but only as long as they can see us."

As usual they took the most direct route across country, some of which was owned by squatters. These men rarely complained seeing the police cross their land as it indicated to those who had an eye to do a spot of stealing, to go elsewhere for the day at least until it was safe again.

Sunny Flat was beside water at the bottom of a high hill, John had been to this community a few times and was looking forward to seeing his friends.

"Sergeant Greg Knox is at the barracks and we'll be welcome to stay there, but we'll have to invent some story as to why we've come down to this community," he said to Willie.

"How long has it been since you were here last?"

"Not for a few months, it has developed into a thriving community since I came here about eighteen months ago."

"What caused it to thrive so well?"

"A few miles out of the settlement is a large property, which employs lots of men and shepherds, it's done very well with a large flock of sheep."

"I suppose we'll have no problems in discovering what Sergeant Green wants to know?" Willie asked carefully.

"I've been thinking about this problem and I want you to wander about the community and remember to be cautious. While you are seemingly just a visitor, I'll be asking questions"

"My part is to be keeping a look out for trouble while you're asking questions."

"Yes that's what's in my mind. In the meantime come and meet Mrs. Hunt."

They rode down the main road of the community to a solid-looking building constructed of bricks with a sign read Victoria Inn.

"That sign is new," John smiled and said.

They alighted and tied their horses to a long hitching rail under a tree. Willie followed John into the building to be cheerfully greeted by a well-dressed middle-aged woman, who gave John a big hug. Willie was made equally welcome as an older man walked out of a nearby room and John greeted him.

"Back teaching, Mr. Hunt?"

"Yes John, and most satisfying it is too."

They followed Mrs. Hunt through to a large room filled with tables and benches, a young girl was putting plates on a table and looked up and seeing John she gave a cry of joy and hurried across the room to give him a big hug. Willie watched with a smile and was soon greeted by the girl called Betsy. A young man came into the room wearing a long apron and greeted John.

"Meet Bob Pringle, he is an ex-policeman." John said, turning to Willie.

"Cooking is a much safer occupation," Bob explained.

"After hearing some of the stories from your kitchen experiences with Betsy, retold by Tom and Dick, I'm not so sure about it being a safe place!!" John replied and laughed.

Everyone laughed as Bob put an arm around Betsy's shoulder, John saw her smile at Bob and was satisfied that the relationship was solid.. Undercover of the family humour, Mrs. Hunt said quietly to John, "I suppose you're here for gathering information about a certain matter."

"Yes Mrs. Hunt, where is a safe place to talk?"

"In the kitchen when we're washing up. We've been aware that there have been some odd-looking characters in our community of late."

"Willie can go for a walk around the community and have a look at it," John suggested.

"Not on his own John, it may not be safe, Bob can go with him."

"Surely it isn't as bad as you're suggesting."

"Recently since Dick had that encounter, the local police are on edge. Dick will be back tonight and you can talk to him. With so many sounds in the kitchen no one will hear you talking."

While they were talking Willie was surprised to see an unknown Sergeant of Police walk in and be greeted cheerfully by the Hunt family. John turned and introduced Willie saying, "This is Sergeant Knox, Mr. Darkwood."

"Glad to meet you Mr. Darkwood, I've come to have a word with Mr. Hale. Do you mind if we go for a walk Mr. Hunt?"

"Feel free Sergeant Knox."

He smiled and guided John out of the Inn, saying , "I've had a note from Sergeant Green and I know why you're here. Officially you will create another reason for this visit, do you understand Mr. Hale?"

"Yes Sergeant."

"I've had some strange police appointed to my barracks and I can't be sure of your safety in my district. I'd suggest you find out what you need to know and leave as quietly as you can during the night."

"We were intending to stay at your barracks tonight."

"No. Not safe, if you can get your information, go tonight."

"Are the Hunt family safe?"

"I hope so Mr. Hale."

"We'll leave as soon as it's safe to go."

"Warn that boy of yours to be extra careful, he isn't safe either, not here."

"In full daylight?"

"At any time Mr. Hale."

John walked back into the Inn and gave the warning to Willie, who was inclined to laugh at the idea that he wouldn't be safe on the road in full daylight.

Mr. Hunt who had been close enough to hear John's words explained, "Mr. Darkwood I have learned that on the frontier, any time can be dangerous, surely as a policeman you know what I'm talking about in a settlement like this one."

"Yes Mr. Hunt, but this appears to be a safe community," Willie replied, catching a speaking glance from John.

"It's still a remote community Mr. Darkwood."

Bob and Willie left the Inn. An hour later Bob returned with torn clothes and dried blood on his face saying, "We were attacked outside the general store by two men with clubs, they took Willie away and I couldn't stop them, I've never seen the two men in this community before today."

His face was white in shock as he drew a breath and continued, "I tried to follow as they took him behind the stables, I did get close enough to see two of the new police sitting on a bale of straw, as one of the men questioned Willie." He added, "Willie was refusing to speak and they were using a stick on him."

"Betsy, dry your tears, pull yourself together and run across the road and tell Eddy Redwood to get some fellows together and rescue Willie, go now." Mr. Hunt spoke sternly.

Betsy took one look at her father's face and ran out of the room.

"Eddy Redwood is the blacksmith and is one of our best customers along with his friends," Mrs. Hunt explained.

Half an hour later Willie was brought into the Inn by a group of strong young men, a couple showed evidence of a fight, and the man John identified as Eddy spoke, "This is a bad business. Sergeant Knox came with us and witnessed the two police directing the assault on Mr. Darkwood. He has arrested them. They put up a fight but were no match for my friends."

"Mr. Hale the Sergeant wants a word with you now, please," One of the young men said.

John left by the washing-up room doorway into the back yard to find the Sergeant sitting on an old stump to one side, out of sight of anyone walking past the Inn.

"I did warn you. You must be out of Sunny Flat before sunrise, I can't hold the police in the lock-up any longer than early morning. One of those strong young men managed to get a name from one of the men with the stick."

"Who was it?"

"Inspector Jimmy Straw, John Sefton's brother-in-law. This a nasty business."

"Do you think he's behind the attack on John Sefton?'

"No, I'd say there's someone else behind him. That's not to say Straw has clean hands, he's obviously involved."

"Was there anything else discovered by our enterprising young men?" John asked.

"No. They wanted to know what you were doing down here. Your boy remained silent and took a nasty beating, but no bones are broken."

"We'll leave Sunny Flat as soon as I get the information I came to receive today," John said, expressing his appreciation to Sergeant Knox.

They parted company understanding the precarious position each of them had taken in working together in this current situation. Secrecy was essential and John would play his part as soon as he'd spoken to Dick. He walked back into the Inn and a few minutes later, the Sergeant exited through the back entrance.

Mrs. Hunt and Betsy were attending to Willie and told John, "Go away."

He was only too pleased to obey and found the young men with mugs of ale in their hands.

"We have been talking about Mr Darkwood, he's in no condition to ride a horse, not tonight, but we know you have to leave before dawn," Mr. Hunt said, handing him a mug.

"What do you suggest we do?" John asked, knowing Mr. Hunt and his ability to organise things.

"I've just told these men that you were at one time one of my students, and that they would have no problem with you. Mr. Redwood has a plan, so listen to him." Mr. Hunt said.

John saw the expressions on the faces of the young men and smiled in complete understanding, as Eddy spoke quietly, "My brother has a small wooden hut outside Sunny Flat, on your way north of here. He, with the help of a couple of us, will take Mr. Darkwood and his horse as soon as it's dark to the hut. It's position is well protected by trees and it can't be seen until you actually ride up to it."

Who do I thank for this plan?" John asked.

"No names please, this dangerous work. Dick knows where it is and will bring you later tonight," Eddy replied, then added, "I will come and bring supplies in the morning. Mr. Darkwood won't be able to ride a horse for a couple of days. He's barely conscious at the present time."

"Very well, I accept your kind assistance and will see you in the morning."

John walked out of the room and found his way into the back room where Willie lay covered in bandages and looking sorry for himself, was barely awake.

"Willie nod if you can hear me," John said to him.

He nodded in a slow movement which was obviously painful.

"Good boy, now listen."

John explained what the plan was to be tonight and why it was necessary to move him, when he was in so much pain. Willie nodded his understanding and drifted back to sleep. He didn't wake up when the men came to move him. Nor did he awake as he was driven in a dray over rough ground to the distant hut. One of the men remained following Mrs. Hunt's instructions, he'd brought his own swag and rations. He smiled knowing why the hut had been built and what the young men used it for on many nights in secret!! It wasn't for other men either. He was happy that Eddy's brother offered it to the police, out of a deep respect for Mr. and Mrs. Hunt. Both Tom and Dick had used this hut at times too. It would be a long night looking after this man and not enjoying the delights of his usual companion here.

✳

Dick Hunt arrived home after dark and greeted John like a long-lost brother, as he always did when the saw each other, after all they had known one another almost all their lives.

"I was coming home a few weeks ago and getting close to Sunny Flat, when I saw a dray being ransacked by two men. As I approached the dray they ran away. I stopped and looked to see any identification on it, and hearing a sound, I turned to see a middle-aged woman crawl out from under a nearby bush. She was in a bad way with a torn dress and was generally dishevelled with leaves and small sticks clinging to her clothes. I helped her put as much as I could, trying to find her property and put it back on the dray and took her to my

Mother's Inn. She told me she was being hunted by evil men. I instantly knew her identity and kept quiet, she was able to pay for her own room.

"After she had cleaned herself up, I took her to the small area behind the washing-up room, she looked surprised and I explained that there was someone else who was being hunted by evil men here. She walked out the door and saw who was sitting on a stump, all doubts vanished as I heard John say 'Susie you're here. They are closing in on us and I know a place where we can be safe.'" Dick continued, "I stored her belongings in my shed, she left her horse and dray with me. They had gone in the morning and no one saw them leave Sunny Flat."

John and Dick talked about where they had gone after leaving Sunny Flat, neither knew and it became another mystery. Dick took John to the hut. John laughed when Dick told him how the young men and himself used this precious building on many nights in the warmer months!!

Chapter 10

As usual in the Victoria Inn washing up room, it had been a busy day with making extra meals for a large group of bullock dray drivers, taking a large consignment of goods to a distant place. Bob Pringle, ex-policeman now for almost eighteen months, looked forward to creating an interesting menu during the day in the company of the beautiful Betsy. She would be his wife soon and he looked forward to that day. When no one was in sight they greeted each other with a kiss in the mornings. Before going to their separate rooms at night there was another hug and kiss, depending upon how much time they had alone. Bob obeyed the rules of their courtship. Betsy's three older brothers watched him and enjoyed his discomfort, knowing full well what was in his mind on most days! His respect for Mr. and Mrs Hunt kept him from further exploration when he was alone with Betsy.

The Hunt family thought he was out of the police, and it was true to a certain extent. He'd joined the police because the man who lived next door to his parents cottage thought he might do well in it. His name was John Sefton, but it soon became obvious to both of them that the police career was not a suitable one for Bob. That friendship remained and grew with the years. When the dark clouds began to gather over the head of John Sefton, he contacted Bob, knowing he had an excellent solution to his problem of where he could be safe, until the storm clouds had been vanquished and he could come out of hiding.

A couple of months before the storm broke out, Bob had taken leave from cooking to search for native herbs to add flavour to Betsy's dishes. He was away for several weeks. Unknown to the Hunt family, he left on a horse and about four miles out of the community, rode to a farm. He changed to a dray filled with building materials, plus two men. They wanted work to pay for their trip down to the gold fields near Melbourne.

"There is a hut to be repaired in an out of the way location and water barrels to be filled a good distance from water," Bob had explained.

The men agreed with the payment offered. The hidden place was two days out of Sunny Flat. While the men worked and repaired the hut and filled the ware barrels, Bob planted seeds of various vegetables in a garden, which had been overgrown since he'd last seen it. When they left it was a good dry hut and all signs of the previous unfortunate couple removed. The path that had been leading to the hut was covered in branches and no sign of it remained. Bob had left hooks and the left-over slabs of wood, when the time came they would need to protect their rations from ants, and other forms of life. The wildlife, small enough to creep into cracks, would see the rations as a bounty of riches to be devoured if possible!

At the farm they received their wages and continued south to other riches. Bob paid the farmer, collected a bag of native herbs and rode back to Sunny Flat. Betsy was delighted with the bag of herbs and they added a wonderful flavour to her favourite meat dish. Bob explained where he had found them to her delight. So the weeks passed, until late one afternoon, when he was washing up plates and mugs, the cooking shed, which was out the back of the building, caught fire. No other part of the Inn burned down. The back door opened and Bob looked up from a tub of mugs, to see who was coming in and saw Dick Hunt.

"Bob, there's an old man out in the shed, give him something to eat and drink please," he said.

There was something in Dick's manner which conveyed to Bob to make it a good meal, not like what they usually gave to the hungry people, providing they continued to walk out of the community. Bob filled the mug with ale and a full plate of food and walked out to the shed, opened the door and saw the man.

"No names Bob," he said quietly.

"You made it in one piece!" Bob smiled happily.

"It was touch and go at times."

"Does Dick know you by your real name?" Bob asked.

"Yes, he and Tom have done work for me."

"They are safe."

"Good men."

"You'll be safe here for a couple of days."

"Bob, I'm expecting a friend, remember no names!"

Bob smiled and said gently, "She's not here yet."

"So you know about her too?"

"If you remember, you once sent me to her with a message. She gave me a mug of tea and we talked for an hour or so."

"I'm glad you are engaged to be married," He grinned and said adding, "How are you going to move us from Sunny Flat?"

"There is an old man who at one time was a clown. He will make you up in such a way that no one will recognise you, even those who know you both very well. I have two horses in poor condition, which no one will want to steal, also a broken-down dray for the same reason. You will both use sticks to walk and you will be of a different shape. Get the picture?"

"Bob you are wasted as a cook," the man laughed quietly.

"It's what I want to be. Listen, they are searching everywhere for you, the alert is high red. I'll be happy to see you on your way as soon as she arrives."

"Bob, when we have gone, will you please send a message to Sergeant Norm Green, saying only "We are both safe.""

"I will," adding, "Are you happy with the policeman I will use to convey your message?"

"Yes, he's an excellent choice Bob."

The man ate his meal with a deep satisfaction of his faith in his friend Bob Pringle, while the man in question returned to washing up a pile of plates.

Chapter 11

John finished his mug of ale and asked, "Dick, do you have any idea where they've gone to?"

"No, but I do hope they'll be safe."

They talked as they rode out of Sunny Flat to the distant hut. In the darkness John was unable to see Dick's expression and was unable to gauge whether he was telling the truth or not. Dick knew this is what John was thinking and laughed.

"What are you making merry over Dick?" John asked.

"You, John. I'm telling you the truth, this is too serious a job to make errors. We are fighting unseen men and we have to win."

"If you don't know Dick, then who else in Sunny Flat organised their escape, because no one saw people described like them were leave the community."

"You're forgetting Bob Pringle, he's an ex-policeman."

"He's a cook," John laughed and replied.

"John, both Tom and I have slowly come to realise that Bob Pringle isn't just a cook, and we're glad our sister has chosen to marry him. You're right, he is a cook but a lot more besides creating lovely food," Dick said thoughtfully.

"What makes you think this, Dick?"

"We are now talking secrets John."

"I'd rather you didn't tell me anything which I can't repeat to Ian Percy, for example."

"Why John?"

"To all intents and purposes you're my brother."

"I understand John, and I won't burden you either."

As it turned out John never learned until it was all over that Bob Pringle had received messages at night and Dick believed that his future brother-in-law had played a major part in helping John Sefton and Susie escape and find a refuge in absolute safety. Both Tom and Dick regarded Bob Pringle as someone special, with unknown depths.

*

Willie slept until quite late in the morning and didn't feel a happy boy at all, with aches and pains all over his body, even the slightest movement was painful, but lying still all day wasn't to be endured either. When both his nurse and John were outside, he gritted his teeth and gradually began to move this way and that way. After a couple of days, he managed to stand and hobble out into the sun. Both men looked around in surprise and smiled.

"When can I ride my horse?" Willie asked.

"Not until you can mount and dismount, then you can ride your horse," John replied.

At his request, each day was one of constant pain, but he refused to give into his agony. He exercised at every opportunity and when he fell there was more blood which needed attention. Still. he pushed ahead until after four days he could mount his horse and dismount on his own.

"When this problem is over, will you come and drink a jug of ale with me in Sunny Flat?" The young man they called Rex smiled and said to Willie.

"Yes I will Rex."

Before he mounted his horse he turned to Rex and thanked him. To Rex's surprise Willie gave him a gentle hug of appreciation, saying, "This one is from me, you gave me lots to keep me moving."

Willie mounted his horse carefully. There was still pain, but he was going back to Hill Top.

Chapter 12

As John and Willie commenced their patrol, half an hour later Charley Rush, Alf Stokes and Barry Hodge rode out of the police horse yard and turned south with enough rations for a few days. They talked about each other's life experiences as they rode down south.

"Alf what caused you to join the police?" Charley asked.

"I was in the army for a time, but it didn't appeal to me. I wanted the Mounted Police because I love horses and also in the bush the unity is strong. The problem is showing who the real men are in our unit at Hill Top."

"I agree the unity is vital to a successful barracks, it would be a disaster if each man was on his own," Charley commented.

Charley had remembered in the operation of the closed valley, Alf had talked about his army career and given some ideas which had been a great help at the time. Charley noted that he rode sitting up straight, black beard neatly trimmed and eyes alert. He smiled and Alf asked, "Satisfied?"

"Yes Alf, you'll do, this a bad business and I'm not looking forward to facing Roy and Steve."

"We need to keep them as far away from the actual events as we possibly can," Alf suggested.

"Not easy Alf, when the guns are facing in their direction."

"No," adding "They're safe with us."

The first night camp went well until the morning, when Barry wanted to talk and only received grunts from Alf, which set the tone for the remainder of the day and into the evening. Just after they'd made their fire to cook their evening meal three men on horses rode up to the camp.

"Where are you fellows headed?" they asked.

Charley and Alf gave non-committal answers, but the visitors made no move to go away and Barry who was fed up with Alf said without thinking, "If you must know we're going down to "Red Lands" now go away."

"Why are you going to "Red Lands"?" One of the men asked.

Barry, who wasn't looking at his colleagues who were desperately trying to catch his attention, replied, "To talk to Roy Cook."

"What about?"

"Barry not another word," Alf said loudly.

"You wouldn't say a word this morning," Barry said angrily, then turned to the man on the horse, said, "I don't know."

Both Charley and Alf were almost white with fury. The men took one look at their faces and decided to leave.

As the men rode away Barry began to prepare the meal. Unseen by him, Charley gripped Alf's arm and whispered, "Not now, we're going to have to talk on our own later tonight."

"What's the matter with you, those men have been following us since we left Hill Top," Barry said looking up at them.

"You could have shared that knowledge with us before now," Charley said calmly.

"I've been told you're protecting a criminal and those men on horses are good men," Barry said, fuming.

"Barry that's a lie, whoever told you that lie is definitely at fault," Alf replied.

"You would say that to protect yourself," Barry said, who was still cross about Alf not talking.

He turned away to put the quart-pots on the fire. They ate the meal in silence and Barry went to his swag feeling miserable. He wished he had his friend Bernie here. As soon as he was seen to be asleep. Charley began packing up the camp with Alf helping to move as quietly as possible.

"Which of us will cause the others to return to Hill Top?" Charley asked.

"Can you do it, if you can, play up loudly and we'll leave in the moonlight before dawn?" Alf answered.

"Okay, what do you suggest?"

"Pains in the belly will be most believable."

"Whatever, we can't go on to "Red Lands". Barry doesn't think before he speaks, a bad habit in a policeman, one day it will get him into a lot of trouble."

They left the camp before dawn and rode well into the next night. Charley put on a magnificent performance and later Alf congratulated him as they drank a pot of ale together. Sergeant Green sent an urgent message to Red Bryant with the details of the break in confidence.

After a reasonable time had elapsed and Barry was out on another job with Bernie Sharp, Alf and Charley gathered rations and quietly left for "Red lands", the new name of Red Bryant's property beside the ranges.

Alf and Charley talked as they rode down the well-used track before turning east cross open country, preferring to travel on their own away from the men travelling between gold fields. So began their ride down to Red Bryant's property now called "Red Lands". As usual it was a long ride and they enjoyed conversing on all kinds of subjects. Alf commented upon Barry's petulant behaviour that he determined to be unacceptable in a policeman of any age.

"Why are you smiling?" Alf asked.

"I heard a story that Barry went to the horse yard and saw a good-looking horse, saddled it without asking the farrier, and rode out on a job for a couple of hours. On returning he received a sharp lecture for taking the Inspector's horse!"

Nothing impeded their journey and Charley was interested to see the new red sign at the entrance to Red Bryant's land. There were all kinds of improvements with the main house now constructed out of bricks, a big difference from the original wooden slab huts, which were inclined to leak water when the rain was heavy. Now the roof on each brick building was made of wooden shingles and looked impressive.

Red came out of his house to greet the two policemen, followed by his wife Mary. After the greeting they followed the man with the red beard back into the house and were given mugs of tea.

"Were you visited by three men on horses, a few weeks ago, who gave you an uneasy feeling?" Charley enquired.

"Yes we did see them. I was able to tell them I hadn't seen you."

"Did they ask anything about Roy?"

"Yes they asked, and I told them I hadn't seen him for some weeks. I suggested they try Alan Gill at "River Oaks", because that is where Roy was most likely to be."

"That was clever Red," Charley said and laughed.

"I wasn't born yesterday Charley!"

"Did they go down to the Gill land?"

"No."

Any idea of their identities?"

"Not sure, but bad men, properly connected to William Knox."

"What did they want with Roy?"

Red spoke quietly, "Roy is on a death list."

"One of those men needed to be able to identify him," Charley suggested.

"Where is Roy?" Alf asked.

"Talking to Kevin in the milking shed, they get on well together," Red said and smiled.

"Kevin from the closed valley?" Charley asked.

"Yes, he's become a real asset to us in looking after the cows, they follow him and Mary dotes on him because she doesn't have to do the milking anymore!" Red grinned.

"Have you heard anything about Ken Taylor, he used to work for me during his training before going to the closed valley?" Red asked Charley.

"Steve's had a couple of letters from him. He's returning to work on a special assignment . No details are known."

"Are Roy and Steve available for a private conversation which we would like to remain in this room?" Charley asked.

Steve and Roy arrived, filled their mugs with tea and waited for Charley to speak.

"Your Adoptive Mother has disappeared and we have no idea where she is at the present time," he informed them quietly.

Steve and Roy remained silent.

Charley had expected some response, not total silence so he continued, "We discovered she sold her Tea Rooms and bought a dray and two horses. We know a note was hand delivered to her to get out of the city quickly. One of our men made discreet enquiries and was amused to find out she drove her dray at night from one hotel stable to another, all friends of hers and of John Sefton. No one saw her leave the city and she crossed the Nepean River by punt early one morning, and vanished."

Steve and Roy remained silent and Charley asked with a slight tone of irritation in his voice,

"You do understand what I've just said don't you?"

"We heard you Charley, what do you want us to say?" Roy replied.

Alf in a baffled tone of voice added, "If this was my Mother, I'd want to know what had become of her."

Steve glanced at Roy and gave a nod.

"Our Adoptive Mother is highly intelligent, if she had wanted us to know she would've told us. We are satisfied to leave her alone to conduct her own business," Roy said.

"Charley, Alf, I'd forget about it if I were you. Susie knows how to look after herself, she's been doing it for years," Red laughed and explained.

"There's another matter Sergeant Green asked me to bring to your attention. It's about the paper work concerning your Grants of land. Where are they at the present time?" Charley said sighing.

"Mine are in the keeping of Alan Gill, my future father-in-law," Roy replied.

"Can you trust him?" Alf asked.

"He's Anne's father, of course I trust him."

Alf nodded to Steve who replied, "In a safe place along with Ken Taylor's papers."

"Have either of you started to build or use your land in any way," Alf enquired.

"Mr. Gill and Victor run cattle on my block. We have begun to build a couple of slab huts on Steve's block, close to the border of Red's land," Alf enquired.

"I have leased both Steve's and Ken's block for the time being," Red added.

"Why are you building on Steve's land first?" Charley being curious asked.

Roy smiled and replied, "Just feel like it Charley, just feel like it."

"I do hope you can trust Mr. Gill," Alf said to Roy.

"So do I Alf."

Charley and Alf left the next morning for Hill Top. Both men were uneasy, something didn't feel right.

"Willie told me that both Steve and Roy are highly intelligent. I'd suggest they know exactly what they are doing," Alf commented.

Chapter 13

Bob Pringle was aware that he'd need to pass on the message from John Sefton, but he felt it would be better to let some weeks pass before he made a trip to Hill Top. The assistant blacksmith who helped Willie get his strength back in the hut, whom they'd called Rex, had been impressed by Willie's courage. He'd had a long conversation with John Hale, with the result that he later approached Sergeant Knox to ask about joining the police. It was known he loved horses, was unmarried and was not going out with anyone, though he was popular with the local females. When he discovered that Bob Pringle was an ex-policeman, he visited him often to ask questions. The result was that Rex Howard was sent to the city for training with a note to say he was expected at Hill Top at the end of it. The only comment made by Eddy on hearing he was to lose his assistant, was to the effect that he might have a better chance with the girls now that Rex was out of the running!.

The Hunt family were shocked to receive Ian Percy's note. Tom was inclined to disregard it, but Dick insisted he take care in what he did in his jobs, saying, "The least they know about our work, the less we have to fear."

Tom listened, he liked both his men and couldn't believe one would betray him. So he did nothing. Bob waited until Dick had a reason to go up to Hill Top, then asked if he may accompany him.

"Why do you need to go up to Hill Top?" Dick asked.

"I've contacted Bill Todd to find me a quantity of native herbs for Betsy."

"That means I will be bringing back bags of stinky stuff in my clean dray, does it?" Dick laughed.

"Very likely Dick!"

"We'll leave as soon as I have a full load booked, I'm waiting to hear from a person who is moving up to Hill Top."

This plan suited Bob because he didn't want to be on the road at the same time as the two city policemen. It was five days later, when Dick told Bob to be ready the next morning before sunrise. They had a good trip, travelling at a fast rate with four horses. Bob found himself watching Abe and Jack and wondering which man had betrayed Tom?.

Bob was delighted with the several bags of herbs which Bill had located for him. Later in the day Bob managed to get Bill and Ian on their own after their meal. They had wandered over to a couple of logs under a tree and sat down to talk generally about Sunny Flat, being curious about what had happened after the attack on Willie. Bob was able to tell Ian and Bill about Rex and that the blacksmith had a new assistant.

"My visit to Hill Top was at the request of an Inspector, to pass a message to both of you. I am commanded to deliver the words only and not elaborate upon them, I do hope you understand. The message is not to be revealed to anyone, this includes Sergeant Green," Bob said quietly.

Bob had their entire attention and satisfied spoke almost in a whisper, "The words are: "We are both safe now." I do hope you understand."

"Are you able to say a name?" Ian asked.

"Knowing I am unable to say another word on this subject?"

"Yes, we both hear you Bob, just the name," Bill replied carefully.

"John Sefton."

Bob knew these two men very well, he could see questions being formed in both their minds, then being discarded, at last Ian asked, "How do you know him?"

"Who do you think encouraged me to join the police?" Bob smiled and answered, adding, "The matter is now closed."

Ian, as Bob expected, wanted more information.

"It's too risky Ian, what if you talk in your sleep after a night in the lower tent, a girl might make the right conclusion of a few words," Bob smiled and answered.

Ian was indignant and was about to speak, when Bill laughed and said cheerfully, "I wouldn't go down that path, Ian, not if you remember what happened last time!!"

Ian looked at his grinning friend and said to Bob, "I take your point."

Glancing at Bill with a question in his eyes. Bill seemed to understand and asked, "Bob, we don't understand, you're not a policeman any longer"

"Really!" Bob smiled and replied quietly.

A call from Dick Hunt and Bob shook hands with his friends, walked to his horse and followed Dick out of Hill Top and down the track to Sunny Flat.

Chapter 14

John and Susie had driven the old dray out of Sunny Flat in full sight of everyone, even people who knew John walked past him without the slightest flicker of recognition.

"I should have used make-up at other times Susie," John mused.

Susie smiled. Their trip to the ranges took four days of the gentle plodding of their ancient horses, who required periods of rest. Bob Pringle was quite correct, no one wanted to steal the horses. Men came up to look at them as possible mounts, and at the old dray too and decided to leave them alone.

At the base of the hill in the ranges, John and Susie alighted and led their horses up the path. It wound steadily upwards around the hill gradually rising until the path reached a flat area. The dray had carried all their worldly possessions, plus piles of rations for a long stay. Mrs. Hunt had seen to their requirements saying, "Bob can take other rations to you or whatever else you need living in the wilderness."

The top of the hill had magnificent views over the tops of other hills in the distance. In the west there was a high hill with thick undergrowth. While Susie examined the slab hut, John saw the vegetable garden full of maturing vegetables. Walking across the top of the hill, he saw an enclosed area suitable for their horses. Beside it was a gully coming down from the higher hill, and he noticed that Bob had created a dam, a little to one side of the main stream, so a great rush of rain water coming down from the higher hill wouldn't destroy the dam wall. It was full of water and a channel had been cut, so it flowed through to the enclosure to the horses.

John returned to the hut and told Susie about all that he'd seen and how thoughtful Bob Pringle had been in making this hide-out so comfortable for them. They settled into a life style which required constant vigilance for other criminals roaming the ranges. After some weeks John carefully suggested, "Susie we ought to get married."

"We are married if you remember?" She smiled and replied.

John looked decidedly uncomfortable and spoke, "That was a fake marriage"

"Why was it a fake marriage John?"

"It was the only way I could get into your bed Susie."

She laughed, not in the least offended and replied, "That is what your sister Margaret thought, when we talked about it," adding, "John it was a real marriage, you have been my legally married husband for over twenty years."

"You're wrong Susie, it was a fake clergyman."

"It was to be a fake marriage, until Margaret realised what was planned. She swapped the old drunk for a real clergyman, who was addicted to the bottle," Susie laughed and explained.

"What about when you were away for all those months, twice I seem to remember?"

"Having your sons, John."

"So that's what you were doing," He sat still, quite stunned, before saying, "It seems to me that there has been a lot of interference in my life. Steve and Roy?"

"Margaret recognised them as your sons the moment she saw them."

"Do they know I'm their father?"

"Yes dear, I think they have always known, or perhaps only Roy?"

"So we are already married"

"Yes you daft old man, and before you ask, Steve and Roy are fond of you in their own way. Your sons are bright, especially Roy, Margaret says he inherited that gift through your grandmother who grew up in the Highlands of Scotland."

"I'm going to have a lot to say when I next see my sister, how do you know her?'

"We've been friends for years, long before I met you John."

"I suppose I wanted a fake marriage, so I could act like a real husband, whenever I felt like it."

"I played your game, even hiding our children from you, until it went badly wrong," Susie said.

"What happened?"

"The families I put them with had houses side by side, and used my money for their own children, eventually turning Steve and Roy out into the street. I saw my boys looking for food in a garbage bin in a filthy street."

"You took them into your house. Why didn't I know?"

"Women's business John."

John Sefton prided himself on being a clever man, it had slowly dawned upon him that Susie, with the help of his sister, had allowed him to think for over twenty years that Susie was on the game when all the time it was an act, beautifully played. That took intelligence and determination to carry it on for so many years. For a moment he wondered if he ever knew this incredible woman.

"What if I'd got married?" he asked curiously.

"You would've been a bigamist!!"

"I'm married?"

"Yes John, so let's change the subject and talk about something more interesting."

"Like what?"

"Where did those hens lay their eggs?"

Chapter 15

Willie's return to the barracks with John Hale from Sunny Flat was uncomfortable with the questions from his colleagues, also the long session with Sergeant Green.

"I didn't say anything to those F___ bastards at all," he said in frustration.

"How would Willie know what he'd said if he was barely conscious," George Nash, who heard his words, said out loud.

"His word is good enough for me," John Hale replied furiously.

One night in the barracks was more than enough for both Willie and John. In the morning they begged the Sergeant for a job out in the field, anywhere. Their Sergeant was happy to oblige and gave John the details of a patrol.

"Are you well enough for a long day in the saddle?" John asked Willie.

"Even if I wasn't well, one night in that awful barracks with George Nash behaving the way he does to Barry Hodge, is more than I can endure at the present time."

"It isn't good is it?"

"No John. I have no idea how it will end, and I don't want to be here when it does end."

They rode east towards Deep Glen to find a small shanty grogshop on the Lachlan road.

"Why are we going there?" Willie asked.

"It's taken you almost a day and a half to show an interest in our destination," John laughed and replied.

"Just to get out into the fresh air was my desire, I do love the freedom of riding over the landscape. Well, why are we going to a shanty?"

"Our Sergeant heard that your two police stayed there and made themselves unpopular, our Sergeant would like to know anything interesting about their visit. I did hear you say to him 'anything ', so you have it Willie and no complaining."

They found the shanty and it did look like a broken-down shed, dirty with old straw on the floor. The publican wore greasy clothes and wore a long apron, stained by all manner of things, best not to enquire too closely to their origins. His customers were equal in dress to himself and none too clean. John and Willie asked for an ale, which was quite good, much to their surprise.

"He drew it from the other barrel, half hidden, not what he's serving the other men." John whispered.

The other men down the end of the slab of timber, eyed the police warily, drank their ale and walked out almost as if they couldn't get out fast enough!

"Are you from Sergeant Green?" The publican enquired in a different tone of voice.

Surprised, John replied, "We're from Hill Top."

Willie also enquired

"Are you the normal publican here?"

"Now Mr. Darkwood, I can't be answering that question, can I?"

They hadn't been introduced and Willie sat open mouthed.

"Close your mouth boy or something will fly into it!!" the man behind the slab counter said.

"Do we call you Inspector?" John smiled and asked.

"I'd rather you didn't call me by my rank, in case you forgot in front of the wrong people."

"What do we call you?" Willie asked.

"Jason will do all the time please. Tell your Sergeant that I've written a report with all the required details, which you will take back with you. Mr. Hale, no one is to know this shanty is part of a police operation. Neither of you remember me do you?" He smiled and asked.

"No Jason," John replied looking totally mystified.

"The old man who joined you at your camp on your way back from Sunny Flat, you kindly gave him some meat to eat."

"You played your part to perfection, you were an old man on the track," John grinned and said.

"I'm pleased to see you doing so well Willie, being beaten up isn't pleasant."

"What happened to those city police?" Willie asked Jason.

"They camped with a group of unsavoury people like themselves and when they awoke, all their property had been stolen. Which included their horses and identity papers. With no money they had to walk back to Penrith."

"Did the contents reveal anything new which we didn't know?" John enquired.

Jason smiled and looked at Willie before saying, "They did carry a report concerning their visit to Sunny Flat, and the mild interrogation of W. Darkwood as being unsatisfactory."

"I hope they enjoyed walking," Willie said cheerfully.

"I don't think so, they'd lost their boots!!" Jason grinned and explained.

Willie laughed and in that instant, and forgetting Jason's rank, gave him a hug in sheer enjoyment at this news of their discomfort.

Dawning on him suddenly, he became embarrassed, until Jason said in a kindly voice, "Don't be uncomfortable Willie, when I read what they'd done to you they were lucky they didn't lose all their clothes too. I took their uniforms, they had their under clothes to walk home in, to the laughter of all who passed them on the road."

They left after a couple more ales out of the right barrel, and their word that the shanty was a secret.

"This place attracts bad men and it's good to know where they're heading and if warnings have to be sent," Jason explained, adding quietly, "In time you'll know why we're running this vital shanty. Keep an eye out please for Jamie Tyson, he works with me."

"We will Jason."

On their way back to Hill Top, after camping a night near water, they came across a lone horseman, who on their questioning revealed his name to be Jamie Tyson.

"I'm lost," he said gruffly.

As they already knew who he represented, introductions were carried out after Jamie had explained, "I'm making for Hill Top."

In the saddle he gave the appearance of being a tall man, with wide shoulders and strong arms, a black beard, neatly trimmed below his chin and dark eyes. Their impression improved after John asked, "Do you talk at breakfast?"

"Yes if the company is good."

"We talk at breakfast too, though some of our colleagues are inclined to be grumpy for the first five hours of the day!" Willie explained.

He laughed fully understanding the usual enjoyment at the beginning of each day.

Chapter 16

Back at Hill Top, while John and Willie saw to their horses, Jamie delivered a bundle of papers to the Sergeant, then after a talk saw to his horse, as Jamie left the office, John and Willie entered. They handed over the papers given by Jason. Sergeant Green was delighted with their observations.

"Our plans are progressing well. Now will you take care of young Mr. Tyson please, he'll be going on a special assignment in a few days' time," the Sergeant explained.

Willie and John walked down to the stables and found Jamie brushing down his horse.

"Jamie, there's a spare bunk near ours if you want it. After you've made your choice of which bed you want to sleep in, we'll take you out for a meal," John suggested.

From the little Jamie had heard, he began to comprehend the conditions at Hill Top barracks were toxic. He wondered how he was going to endure the next few days.

Willie and John took him to Ma Shell's food tent in the early evening. As usual Jamie was appraised and found entirely acceptable as a handsome man. Willie and John enjoyed watching her attention to him and Jamie had no choice but to endure the humour at his expense, all of it good natured, Ma just liked handsome men! The soup put a lining on their stomachs before going to the grog shop. Later, fully tanked, they walked down to the lower tent for much needed relaxation of another kind.

In the morning Jamie discovered just why Willie and John wanted to get out on any patrol to escape the toxic atmosphere of the barracks. There was constant bickering, snide remarks and a general air of distrust, it was a nasty place to be.

George Nash, once a peaceful kind of man, seemed to have crawled out behind this simple attitude to become an unpleasant type of man. No one knew what had caused this change and Bill wondered if a girl had caused it. That this change caused conversation, showed the depth of concern in the barracks. No one liked being in the barracks, but it was home.

Bernie Sharp was of a similar mold and in the middle of the unpleasantness was Barry Hodge who couldn't keep silent, speaking when things were better left unsaid. Many barbs created out of the English language, were used to strike hard and hurt, which Barry didn't seem to be able to ignore. His responses were no match for those swiping at him. Other men not wishing to become involved kept away as much as possible.

Sergeant Green was kept busy in his office with reports to be made to his Senior Staff. These Reports gave the impression that all was well at Hill Top and the city problem had not yet effected the life at the station, which wasn't true. Managing one level of ordinary General Duties on the frontier was one thing, on another level he was attempting to keep abreast of developments concerning John Sefton. In his latest message, the Sergeant had been told that Sefton had been on the brink of arresting a number of police and were to be charged with embezzlement of a considerable amount of money. This was news because everyone thought it had to do with the Grants of land to the boys. Instead the Grants had been the tip of a large pile of greedy men, where enough was never enough. Also in that long communication was a note, not proven, that he had two men reporting from his barracks to the opposition and to be careful.

Sergeant Green was no fool and had realized the contents of the note some months ago. Men who gambled often ran out of money. The desire to play overshadowed common decency or even friendships. The toxic atmosphere in his barracks hadn't been unknown to him for less than a day and he felt a deep concern for his good men having to endure such a home.

Chapter 17

Steve Baker had been constructing a slab hut on his land, above a creek not far from the border of "Red's Land" which was within a hours ride of Red's house. He'd found the work most satisfying and enjoyed Roy's company. Both looked forward to the day they could take their father's name as their own. The uncertainties of their younger years had been washed away after the visit to their Mother.

There was something almost primeval in constructing his own dwelling. Steve still had dreams of Betty Gill and knew this relationship couldn't eventuate until he had his own name. He and Roy spoke quietly about their own dreams. He did feel Roy was keeping something hidden from him. When Steve asked his brother, Roy smirked and explained, "I think we'll have some rough ground to cover before we can settle down to a normal life Steve. I can't see clearly into our future."

They had completed the roof when a message was delivered to Steve late in the afternoon.

"That was well timed Steve, I suppose you'll have to go away again," Roy said cheerfully.

He read the note which had been handed to him and replied, "Yes I do, Margaret Straw, our Aunt, has requested a meeting at Last Stop."

"Who is to accompany you this time?"

"Ken Taylor and a new man called Jamie Tyson, according to Sergeant Green, he added some words to the paper."

"Steve, I believe the trip you're about to make will be the turning point to give freedom to our parents," Roy smiled as if satisfied and said. "You three will be undercover from now on until they are free from having to hide," he added.

"How do you know Roy?"

"Just do."

Steve and Roy spent the first night together in the completed hut and early next morning Steve saddled his horse and rode north. He stopped briefly to see Red, who seemed to know all about the trip to Last Stop and warned him to be careful of strangers at night. He avoided riding anywhere near Hill Top as requested by Sergeant Green and to meet him at a camp area, which Ian Percy would lead him to. Both Bill and Ian had been directed to keep an eye out for him. Once found, Ian took him to the camp and Bill returned to get the Sergeant. No one questioned the Sergeant and Bill going out on their horses. For the last couple of weeks they had been doing this exercise, all in preparation for this meeting.

Bill had been visibly shocked when the Sergeant had stated near the camp, "Bob Pringle is a clever man and I'm pleased to know they are both safe. We're beginning to fight back as many good city policemen have come over the Blue Mountains undercover, we're no longer alone, though at times it may feel like we are."

Bill stayed on one hill keeping an eye out for strangers and Ian rode to the other hill, while the Sergeant rode down to the camp and found Steve having a mug of tea. He removed his own quart-pot from beside his saddle, and Steve went to the creek and filled it with water. The men sat in silence as the water boiled and a small quantity of tea leaves were dropped into the boiling water. Steve gave it a couple of minutes before pouring it into a cold tin mug.

"I know you and your brother visited your Mother and I know what transpired over those couple of days. What you need to know is that your Father is directing the current operation from their hide-out," the Sergeant said after his first sip of tea.

Steve sat quietly holding his mug of tea in both hands, giving the Sergeant his attention.

"At Green Hills or near it you will meet up with Ken Taylor and Jamie Tyson, you three will operate together until the operation has been completed and the men involved arrested. One last detail, you will be under the orders of your Father," he continued.

"Will I see him?" Steve asked quietly.

"Yes, though you may not recognise him, yes you will see him," The Sergeant smiled and almost laughed.

"We are to visit my Aunt and then what?" Steve enquired.

"She will give you some papers, which you will give to your Father and no one else, is that understood."

"Yes Sergeant. Will we be meeting again?"

"If we do meet it will be secretly, no one is safe at the present time. You know Red Bryant and if you are at Sunny Flat, Bob Pringle, the cook at the Victoria Inn, will help you."

The Sergeant stood up and removed a quantity of rations from his saddle bag, including meat and said, "You may need some extra food, you're facing long days in the saddle. On this job you will not have time to hunt for food. Also, you must try hard not to draw attention to yourselves, it's vital those papers get to your Father."

He mounted his horse, looked down at Steve and said, "Mr. Sefton I wish you well."

He turned his mount and rode towards the hill where Bill was waiting.

Steve stood and watched him leave with visible emotion in his eyes. Cleaning up the camp, he mounted his horse and rode north.

He met up with Ken with a hug, they were brothers for life after their experience in the underground creek, escaping from the Closed Valley. Jamie Tyson was of an easy-going personality and both Ken and Steve accepted him as part of the unit, treating him like a third brother. As Sergeant Green had indicated they did have long days on the saddle.

After reaching Last Stop and getting directions to Richard Stafford's farm, Jamie enquired, "Ken, how do you find your way, when all the hills and valleys look the same?"

"If you look carefully Jamie they are all different, we look for land marks, like the lie of the land, unusual trees, all kinds of identifying aspects of the land and valleys."

Jamie asked questions and both men answered, realising he had to know how to look after himself if for some reason he became separated from them.

The Stafford farm was situated on the edge of a wide valley, naturally close to water, with an extensive garden filled with growing vegetables and fruit trees. The fruit trees were close to the water, whereas the brick buildings were above the flood level, on a small rise. They rode to the stables at the back of the house, to be met by a tall man, darkly tanned by long days in the saddle. He was of a sturdy build, probably about five feet ten inches, Ken thought.

"Mr. Stafford?" Steve asked.

"Yes and you'd be Steve Sefton, I believe," he replied.

"Not just yet, Mr. Stafford."

"Perhaps not, your Aunt is my first cousin, so you'd be my second. My name is Richard."

"Thank you Richard, but with my two colleagues, it will be better to remain Mr. Stafford."

He stood still for a moment and said, "I know why you're here. Margaret is Steve's Aunt and I want to be called Richard by all of you, it will be easier. You are engaged in a serious operation, and the least surnames you use the better, I think, for security," accepting Steve's words graciously.

"Do you mean if we're caught and forced to speak, and we don't know your surname, you will be safe?" Jamie suggested.

"Exactly young Jamie."

He welcomed them into his house saying, "My wife and two sons are away in the city visiting family and won't be back while you're here. My cousin is expecting you, she's in a building connected to this one."

"Did you send them away knowing we would be coming here?" Ken asked curiously.

"Yes Ken. This is a nasty business and the least they know about it the better for their wellbeing. I'll be sending Margaret away to a distant friend who will look after her," Richard smiled a little sadly.

"Does that mean you have had men coming to look at the farm?" Steve enquired.

"Yes, and Margaret is to leave after talking to you today." He then added with surprise, "You do know what's happened, don't you?"

"What are you talking about Richard?" Steve replied.

"Inspector Jimmy Straw was found outside the community of Last Stop with his throat cut from ear to ear. He was buried ten days ago."

This was news to the men, as they followed him along the front verandah to the other building where a middle-aged woman was spinning a fleece into a ball of wool. She looked up and remained at her task. Richard introduced each man and they addressed her as Mrs. Straw.

"You are like my brother John was at your age," She said greeting Steve.

"Margaret please get on with it," Richard interrupted.

"Can I take my spinning wheel with me please?" She addressed her cousin.

"Of course, I will take it down to the dray while you are talking to these men.'

"The fleece and balls of wool too please Richard," she added.

"Very well, just get on with it."

She waited until her cousin had left with her spinning wheel and wool and then spoke, "My late husband had a secret pouch in his saddle on the underside. After his body was found all his equipment was brought to me. It was obvious all his clothes had been searched thoroughly, also his saddle bag had been cut up badly. I found the papers which have to go to my brother John." She stopped talking for a moment and continued calmly, "I've written a paper of what I know of the current events and who is involved. My Jimmy betrayed my brother John, but I loved him and I knew they'd kill him once they knew you, Steve, were his blood nephew. Frank Black is believed to have been a close connection with the man who fell into the children's pit with meat ants. Now do you understand Steve?"

Both Ken and Steve looked shocked and Ken spoke passionately, "Not again, not again, please not again."

Steve immediately put an arm around his shoulders and said soothingly, "We have Jamie and lots of other men helping us this time Ken, we won't be on our own, it won't be so bad as last time."

Margaret stood up and put her arms around Ken saying, "I know what you and Steve endured, but Ken you have to know the truth of who you are fighting against in this operation. Knowing is your strength in this battle, you will succeed." She smiled at the three men and continued firmly, "There are three bundles of papers and letters, they are all originals. Each of you will carry a bundle. except Steve who will carry a bundle with a red mark, these you will leave with Andrew Willow at Green Hills." She then asked, "You know where to go with them?"

"Yes Mrs. Straw," they replied.

"Next time we meet Steve, I want to be called Aunt Margaret, is that understood?"

Steve smiled and gave his Aunt a big hug saying, "From Roy and me."

He turned on his heel and walked back down the verandah and said goodbye to Richard.

The three men rode down the valley. Jamie looked back to see a dray and four horses travelling northwards. It was a fast trip to Green Hills and Steve gave the bundle of papers marked in red to Andrew Willow.

They took a wide invisible track away from the usual roads used by men travelling between gold fields, choosing country rarely travelled on the long trip down to Sunny Flat. Near this community they camped with visible views in all directions. In normal times they'd go a distance from the camp for the normal bodily functions, but not on this trip. No one went out of sight of the others. At times it wasn't pleasant, but the stakes were too high to create a problem. As they settled down to boil their quart-pots, they were suddenly joined by two very old men. Instinctively they were on their guard. The old men were instantly aware of the sudden tension around the campfire.

No one spoke until one of the old men asked, "Travelled far?"

"Not far, who are you?" Steve replied.

"We've been waiting for you," he said.

"What proof do you need, for you to believe we are your final destination?" The other old man asked.

"If you are who you claim to be, remove your shirt and let me see that scar?" Steve said.

"Oh dear Steve you can be difficult at times, almost as bad as Roy, but only just'"

He removed his shirt and Steve saw the odd shaped birth mark on his Father's back, except this old man didn't look like his Father.

"I should have known clown make-up on both of you. Is that you Mother?" Steve said

"Yes dear, I couldn't have John wandering around the countryside on his own, could I?" His Mother grinned.

"Your Mother and Father disguised as two ancient men!!" Jamie said in an amazed tone.

"Leave the word 'ancient ' out, Jamie Tyson," Steve's Mother replied grinning.

"You know me?" He asked in a surprised tone.

"Yes dear, your Mother is one of my oldest friends and she told me you were having an adventure, so here you are with two brave men."

They handed over the bundles of papers, as another man arrived.

"It's time to go, we must be back before sunrise tomorrow morning," he informed the old couple.

John Sefton stood up and faced his son saying, "Your Mother has told me everything. It was a terrible shock, but I rather like it. We'll be meeting again, in the meantime you three will continue to work for me. There is another man coming here, go with him, he knows you Steve to be one of my sons. Ken and Jamie you are part of me too so keep safe."

They parted in the twilight after Steve had put out the fire.

Chapter 18

Sergeant Green called Ian and Bill to his office, after they'd eaten the first meal of the day.

"Mr. Percy and Mr. Todd I want you to ride north to meet up with Mr. Willow and Mr. Swan, both Green Hills police, at the usual half way camp, I believe you know where it is," he explained once they were seated.

"Yes Sergeant, we both know it " Ian replied.

"You will be handed some papers which you will believe were in the secret pouch carried by the late Inspector Jimmy Straw. Do you follow me," the Sergeant continued.

"Yes Sergeant"

"On the way home you will be held up and we want the papers to be taken," he continued lowering his voice.

"The papers are false?" Ian said quietly.

"Yes Mr. Percy, they are to lead certain men in another direction, more suitable to our requirements in this operation."

"We understand, we put up a fight, but only enough to give the impression that we're carrying the real papers," Bill enquired.

"Exactly Mr. Todd, I'd like you to take Mr. Hodge with you, it would do him the world of good to get out of the barracks and away from certain individuals."

The Sergeant didn't hear the internal groans, which both Ian and Bill felt at his words, but he did see that their expressions were not hidden fast enough to escape his eagle eyes.

"I hear what you're thinking, you'd prefer to be on your own, but I have my reasons which will later become clear, just be kind to him," he smiled and spoke.

With these words they filed out of the office and called out to Barry who was walking up from the stables.

"Barry, we're going out on a job and you're coming with us, get your horse," Ian said.

He was only too happy to be included in a job with Bill and Ian, because they mostly operated on their own and Barry felt it was a privilege to ride with them. He wasn't aware that George Nash and Bernie Sharp were also interested in why Ian and Bill were taking Barry.

Soon they were out of Hill Top and away on the distant hills, with Barry quite happy to ride behind the older policemen as they crossed the hills on a lovely clear morning.

"Someone's in trouble," Ian said looking down into the valley from the top of a hill. He took out his small brass telescope and said, "There's a native woman cowering behind some low bushes with a small child and down in that gully is a black man doing his best to evade men on horses. We'll ride down and help them."

They carefully rode down into the valley and managed to get close to the woman and child before she looked up and saw them. She didn't move but watch them carefully.

"You stay with her while we go and rescue her man," Ian said to Barry.

Bill and Ian rode down to the gully towards where Ian had seen the black man hiding from the men with guns. Ian rode quietly up to him and indicated silence in the universal way by a finger to his lips. The man looked up in shock when Ian put a bullet into the air This instantly drew the attention of the men who had been further down the gully and hadn't seen the police arrive in the valley.

"Why are you hunting this man?" . Ian demanded.

There was a silence until an older man spoke, "We just kill them on sight."

"You do realise that it's murder and you can go to the gallows."

Ian was no fool and knew the chance of a white man on the frontier going to the gallows was quite remote, so he tried another way to get peace.

"You have a choice to either make friends and learn from these people, who know this land better than you do, or be enemies and live in fear every time you leave your hut to work, leaving your wife and children to face the hatred you have created. The man you were trying to kill was only trying to catch a kangaroo for his woman and young boy," he said.

Ian turned his horse and rode up to where Barry was sitting quietly on his mount beside the man, who was standing a few yards from the horse. He indicated to the native that he was to walk between the horses, up to where his woman was waiting for him.

Meanwhile, Barry looked down from high up on his horse at the woman and child, who was acting bravely at what the guns could mean for his father. He thought of his younger brother who loved tin whistles and had one in his pocket and he'd taught himself to play tunes on it. This one wasn't as good as the one he'd given to his brother and thinking of the pleasure his younger brother had with his tin whistle, Barry alighted from his horse and squatted down near the boy. Both the woman and child watching him intently as he took the whistle out of his pocket and began to play a tune, one after another. Like his brother he saw the boy begin to smile and the fear receded from his face. Barry made himself comfortable on the grass until he heard his colleagues returning with the boy's father. Before standing up, he took the whistle out of his mouth, wiped it on his trousers and gave it to the boy, who took it, Barry then closed his hand around the boy's hand and smiled. The boy returned the smile and showed the whistle to his mother, as Barry mounted his horse and waited for his colleagues. The native had a small kangaroo over his shoulders, walking cheerfully between Ian and Bill. The small family vanished between the undergrowth and the only sounds were bird calls and a tin whistle.

They continued up to the camping area and were joined later in the day by Andrew Willow and Ted Swan. It was a happy time around the fire as Barry relaxed and told some funny stories, which were new to Ian and Bill. In the morning a bundle of papers was handed over into the care of Ian.

"These were found in Inspector Straw's secret pouch under his saddle," Andrew explained.

"That sounds important Andrew," Bill said.

"Yes it is, we've travelled carefully to give them to you, now we can relax on our way home without the responsibility of keeping them safe."

"Don't rub it in!" Bill said, scowling at Ted, who was grinning widely.

They parted in a friendly fashion, after several mugs of tea, before sunrise. The first day was a comfortable ride through a landscape bursting with spring life and camped in a peaceful valley a little away from the usual beaten track.

"We're under observation," Ian whispered to Bill.

"When do you think they'll come?"

"Early in the morning would be my estimate as the best time, before we are properly awake."

Barry was quite contented to make the fire and cook the last of the meat. They were surprised to find that he was a good companion and they enjoyed his company. Ian and Bill were also impressed with his kindness to the small boy. It was almost as if this was a Barry whom they didn't know at all.

In the morning as they finished the first meal of the day and began to pack up, two horsemen rode right into their camp, scattering quart-pots and other items under the horses hooves while two other men arrived on foot, masked and levelled rifles at them. The ransacking began with everything turned out, personal items thrown on to the grass and trampled upon, some were dropped into the fire for fun. Hardly a word was spoken, their horses unhobbled and hunted away out of the grove of trees. At last the papers were located and their property kicked over the ground for good measure. Neither Bill nor Ian spoke a word, only Barry uttered a sound when he was kicked hard in the shins as it had been unexpected the attack on him. The masked men took a last look around the now destroyed camp, laughed and mounting their horses rode across the camp, clutching the bundle of papers, deeply satisfied with the mornings work.

It took most of the day to separate their belongings and catch their horses. This meant another night in the camp. Bill caught a fish and Barry retreated back into his silent world. Ian and Bill did most of the camp work while Barry sat and gazed into the fire.

After their last mug of tea for the night, Barry spoke quietly, "Nothing is what it seems to be in the operation you are conducting at the present time.

If you both want to come out of it in one piece, look beyond the obvious to where truth lies."

With these words Barry bid them good night and went to his swag, leaving his colleagues stunned.

"What did he mean Ian?" Bill asked.

"I think he's telling us something about our own barracks and we're not going to like it."

They rode back to Hill Top in the morning and Sergeant Green complimented the three of them for a job well done.

Chapter 19

Ian Percy felt a hand shaking him on the shoulder and a voice saying with a note of desperation in it.

"Wake up Ian, wake up, please wake up."

Opening his eyes in almost total darkness and remembered he was sleeping in the barracks after a long day in the saddle. He recognised Barry's voice and asked quietly, "What is it Barry?"

"Are you awake?"

'I am now, why have you woken me up in the middle of the night."

"Keep your voice down please."

There was a fear in his voice which Ian couldn't understand, being a compassionate type of man, he asked in a whisper, "What is it Barry?"

"I wanted to tell you that I recognised the three men who held us up yesterday. They were William Knox's men. They told me they'd kill me if I revealed their names to you at the raid. You need to know these are bad men."

Ian instantly wide awake asked, "How do you know them?"

"I saw them in the gaming tent, the night before we rode north."

"I didn't know you played cards."

"I don't play cards for money. I went with Bernie Sharp and George Nash."

"Why did you go with them Barry?"

"A few nights ago I won a lot of money and they took my winnings and lost it all," he said in a whisper.

"Did they offer to pay you back?"

"No Ian, I won't see that money again, not now. It was the only time I've played for money and it was fun for a while, until it became serious."

"But why did you keep going to the gaming tent."

"It was interesting, I just wanted you to know this truth and to be wary in the barracks."

His night visitor vanished into the darkness, Ian was left with the uncomfortable feeling that someone else was awake and had witnessed the conversation.

Chapter 20

Both Charley and Alex spent as many hours as possible away from the barracks, which was quite easy as the Sergeant had many jobs which needed doing, not only with the operation, but ordinary police work on the frontier.

Alex was able to let the constant discord flow over him, whereas Charley was more inclined to pick up the barb and get involved. On some days Alex had to pull him out of the barracks, before there was an eruption, which could easily have got out of hand. Charley being Charley didn't like giving in to bullies. At one lunchtime a fight erupted involving the entire barracks. It had been a long exhausting morning and the men were on edge. It had been a bad beginning to the day and Charley was on cooking duty. George Nash had been even more unpleasant than usual towards Barry who was no match for George at his most cutting in front of his colleagues. Charley had made sandwiches for the men and handed a plate of these to George, who wasn't keen on this type of lunch.

He opened up the two slices of thinly cut damper and looked at the meat saying, "What's this white meat?"

"I thought that this meat and you would be at home together," Charley replied with a straight face.

"What's the F–ing meat?" George looked at the meat and demanded.

Charley grinned and replied as the room fell silent, "Black Snake!"

Suddenly George picked up the sandwich and it sailed through the air in Charley's direction.

"You missed George!" he said ducking.

"You F…ing bastard Rush, one day I'll get even with you, see if I don't."

Red in the face against his black whiskers, he stormed out of the meal room, knocking over a couple of stools and pushing men out of his way, followed by his faithful friend Bernie Sharp. The laughter from the room was the only sound they heard almost to the stables.

"You've made a dangerous enemy today, Charley," Alex told him later.

"I know Alex, he's a bastard if ever there was one."

"I know Charley."

Chapter 21

Ian and Bill sat quietly in the office as their Sergeant completed writing a paper. The glass ink pot was low and not enough ink was attached to the nib at each dip of his pen. At last he placed a sheet of blotting paper over his work.

"I want you two men to go on a fact-finding job and you will need your telescope, Mr. Percy. There is a miners camp at Black Creek north of Deep Glen. You are to observe it from the high hill overlooking the camp. I'd rather you weren't seen at this work, nor that anyone would suspect that an observation has taken place. Do you get my drift?" He said, leaning back in his chair.

"We do," Ian replied.

"There's a grog shanty on the way to Black Creek in the wooded valley before the camp. Make sure they don't see you. I'll be sending Alex Pitt and Barry Hodge to that shanty. In your report from your visit to Deep Glen, you mentioned a camp site some miles from that community?"

"We'd know it again, it had good water and I caught a fish at it!" Bill replied.

"Quite so Mr. Todd," their Sergeant smiled and continued, shifting in his chair as if he needed extra time to gather his thoughts. "At the camp you will be met by policemen whom you will recognise, but do not show in any way that you know them. They will camp at a nearby fire and act as strangers. Only in whispers will you talk as policemen, in all other ways as strangers."

From a shelf beside his desk he took some papers and put them into an envelope and sealed it, saying, "Please remain at this camp until Alex Pitt and Barry Hodge arrive, they will be returning from their visit to the shanty and Mr. Pitt will tell you what they have discovered."

"Do we tell the first group about what we have seen in the miners camp?" Ian enquired.

"Yes, please do Mr. Percy."

"You may hear one of these men address another by a well-known name, show no surprise or ask any questions," the Sergeant moved in his chair again and spoke quietly.

"Are we to return to Hill Top after meeting up with Alex and Barry?" Ian asked.

"Yes in a roundabout route as if you are not carrying anything of importance," he replied before asking, "Mr. Todd I feel you'd like to ask a question but not on this subject and you may do so now."

Bill looked surprised and said, "How do you know?"

"That will be two questions Mr. Todd."

Bill became embarrassed and felt uneasy but was rescued by his understanding Sergeant, who smiled and said, "Please continue Mr. Todd."

"How did you know that Bob Pringle had told Ian and me that they were safe?" Bill took a big breath and asked a little nervously.

Even Ian looked surprised at his friend's question and it showed on his face. The Sergeant knew they had talked about it outside his office, because he'd heard their conversation. He was surprised that Mr. Todd had the courage to ask him an invasive question. He also knew these two men were his best policemen and could be trusted.

"Mr. Pringle is a clever policeman, he knew from firsthand experience of Mr. Percy's and your abilities. Also that you are both highly inquisitive. It was better for all concerned that you knew they were safe, as it would stop you continuing to search for them," He smiled and replied.

"How did you know Sergeant?" Bill dared to ask.

"That is three questions Mr. Todd."

As they stood up to leave their Sergeant replied with a steely expression, "Little birds talk to me Mr. Todd, little birds…"

"But.." Bill began to say, as Ian pulled his arm saying as they exited the office, "If you aren't careful Bill, we'll have a host of difficult jobs for the next month."

"Quite so Mr. Percy, at least two months, if not more than that." their Sergeant grinned and said as they were almost out of the doorway.

"Bill not another word until we are clear of here," he heard Ian say.

"I only asked Ian."

"Bill, he's the Sergeant, you don't ask him invasive questions."

The Sergeant heard Ian's words and smiled, as their footsteps receded from his hearing. He laughed and felt the strength of Bill's question, that determination to know the truth which was a valuable asset in a policeman.

Once out of the office Ian asked, "Bill whatever made you ask that question of the Sergeant of all people?"

"I wanted to know if Bob Pringle is still with the police. Now I'm fairly sure that he is still on the books."

"That's dangerous knowledge Bill, we can never speak about it to Bob or anyone."

"I know Ian. I just wanted confirmation of my thoughts on this matter."

They rode out of the police horse yard and turned east, conversing happily over the long ride to the camp which had a number of ring-barked trees beside a creek. There was no sign that anyone had been there since their last visit and the logs they'd placed to lean against near the fire were still in the same position.

"If we leave here before sunrise, we ought to be in place to overlook the gold mining camp by mid-morning," Ian suggested.

"I wonder why our visit has to be so secret, a gold mining camp is so ordinary," Bill said thoughtfully.

"Bill it's the little birds talking to him again!" Ian laughed quietly.

"F__ing birds."

"Now, now, Bill calm down!"

He received a full mouthful of words and they both laughed quietly. By sun up next morning they were climbing up a tall, wooded hill, riding carefully around steep gullies looking for the tracks where animals crossed them, always climbing upwards to the top and then riding along as quietly as possible so as not to disturb the wildlife which would announce their presence. Blue smoke guided them to the right hill, which was equally wooded as the others they had crossed since leaving the camp. There was no stopping to boil a quart-pot, not until they returned to the camp. They rode along the top of the hill until they reached bare ground with no trees.

"We can't cross this ground on our horses, you stay here with them out of sight and I'll go forward and see what's below us in the valley," Ian said.

Ian left on foot and found a good position where he could use his small brass telescope. He looked down on to what he'd been told was a gold mining camp, to see no such activity taking place in the valley. Whatever was taking place in the valley it wasn't gold digging. He ran his eyes over the valley from end to end and quietly made his way back to where Bill stood with the horses.

"We'll go down the other side of this hill, as quietly as we can and as fast as we can manage," he said in a whisper.

Bill refrained from asking any questions because Ian's voice expressed a fear of something and he'd hear about it later. At the base of the hill they crossed the valley, keeping to the cover of the trees. Never once did they venture out on to the grasslands, always moving at a steady pace. They rode up the other hill and through thick undergrowth, which was difficult for the horses but they couldn't take any chance of being seen by anyone other than the birds. They continued until the blue wood smoke had disappeared into the haze of the morning, though the scent lingered in the air for an hour or so. It was a long ride back to the camp of the ring-barked trees, arriving late in the afternoon. They were rather pleased to see three horsemen already at a campfire a little way from their fire.

"Who do you think they are?" Bill asked.

"Friends Bill, friends," Ian smiled happily.

Ian had not spoken a word since leaving the hill, one look at his face had kept Bill quiet all day. He'd been thinking his friend was afraid of something which he hadn't seen. Now it was a relief to hear a cheerful note in Ian's voice, as they rode into the camp and dismounted. The three other men were wearing ordinary clothes of the shabby style and Bill instantly recognised Ken and Steve and wondered who the other man was to be in such a team. Very quietly he heard him address Steve as "Mr. Sefton."

What came next was too low for Bill to hear clearly. Now he knew and passed this knowledge on to Ian who had just returned from hobbling the horses.

"I'm going down to the creek for a wash, keep an eye out," Ian said.

Steve watched Ian go down through the undergrowth to the edge of the water and followed him.

"Steve the papers which the Sergeant sent to you are under my shirt, put them amongst your clothes and come in for a swim," Ian, who was now in the water, said quietly.

"You can be difficult sometimes Ian, you know I don't want to go into that cold water," Steve spoke in an equally quiet voice.

"No choice Steve, it's the safest place to pass on vital information!"

Ken had followed Steve and collected the papers from under the shirt. He returned to their camp and sat by the now blazing fire. It was late spring and there was still a touch of a winter chill in the night air.

"Steve will need a good fire when he returns from his evening swim," Ken smiled at Jamie and explained.

"In this weather?"

"Yes!"

Meanwhile Ian passed on to Steve a verbal report of what he had seen from the top of the hill.

"I'll race you down the length of the pool, it will warm you up again!" he suggested cheerfully.

"Alright, though I don't ever expect to be warm again."

"Come on swim," he heard Ian say.

They both swam the length of the pool and it was a toss-up who reached the other bank first, as neither would admit to being second. Steve didn't waste time getting dressed by the pool, he grabbed his clothes and went up to his own fire to get dressed in comfort.

"Was it worth the cold?" Ken asked with a grin.

"Yes, Ian had the confirmation we required."

"How close did he get to them?"

"Ian used a small brass telescope from the top of the hill, he saw a camp of men just sitting around doing nothing of anything."

"Did he see our friends who went missing recently?"

"Ian did his best to describe the faces of four men hanging in a tree, further up the creek, they had been brutally tortured before death." Steve spoke sadly.

"I don't think they would've talked, they were strong men deeply committed to John Sefton," Ken said thoughtfully.

"Cook all the meat now, because we'll be leaving here before dawn. We'll ride in the moonlight, we must get this material to my Father. We can eat cold meat riding," Steve told Jamie.

"Two mounted police are coming in this direction," Ken said, looking to the east.

Alex rode around the base of a hill and saw two columns of blue smoke rising from two separate camp fires in the early evening.

"Is this the meeting place?" Barry asked.

"Yes, this is it," adding, "We'll be joining Bill and Ian at their campfire."

Barry didn't enquire as to who was at the other fire, being accustomed to not being told the truth. As usual he observed, which was his gift, not that anyone knew it amongst the police. Not yet. After the usual greetings Alex gave a verbal report to Ian about what he had seen in the grog shop come shanty. It was on top of the hill overlooking the camp below where the gold miners were at work. Alex hadn't asked Barry what he had seen in the shanty. When Alex stopped talking Ian turned to Barry and asked, "What did you see Barry?"

"He was minding the horses." Alex interrupted.

"Yes, I was minding the horses until I saw the hitching rail. There was an outside pit and I walked around to use it, on the way I looked in the back door and saw a man reading some papers, which I recognised," Barry, who liked Ian, replied.

"What were they?" Ian asked carefully.

"They were the papers taken at the hold-up. The man looked up and saw me and smiled. We talked and I showed no interest in the papers, then I continued to the pit and relieved myself."

"You didn't tell me," Alex said with irritation.

"You never asked Alex."

"Anything else Barry?" Ian enquired.

"I'm sure we've been followed since leaving that shanty."

"You're dreaming. Go and check the horses," Alex said unkindly.

"No Alex, I've seen a couple of horsemen keeping at a fair distance behind us."

No more was said on the matter. An hour or so later Barry went down to the creek and passing Ian made an motion with his hand for him to follow.

"I stand between two police operations and neither trust me," Barry told Ian, standing In the moonlight near the water. He held up his hand to stop Ian talking, "Be quiet Ian, we don't have much time so let me speak. I've written out a report of all I've seen or know about your opposition, they are rather nasty people as you have seen with your telescope."

Barry removed a large bundle of papers from under his shirt and gave them to a startled Ian.

"You will need to pass these papers to Steve Sefton to give to his Father," Barry said to a startled Ian. "He will be expecting them Ian."

Ian didn't know what to do. Was this man opposite him was the station fool or he was a very brave man. He didn't even know if he could trust him, he could be a plant by the opposition.

"Who else knows who you say you are Barry?" he asked, trying for time.

"Apart from John Sefton?" He then smiled and added, "Probably Sergeant Norm Green."

"You play a dangerous game of being a fool and saying whatever comes into your mind," Ian said.

"It generally gets to what I want to happen, Charley and Alf reacted perfectly."

"They were furious with you."

"Turning back was what I wanted them to do."

"Anything else we should know Barry?" Ian asked.

"Yes. I'm not sure but I think Alex saw something in the shanty, which is a secret. Alex is a nice man, but he isn't a trained observer, as I am."

"What do you think he saw in that place?"

"I think he saw Frank Black and didn't recognise him."

"So that's why you've been followed here."

"Yes. We'll all have to leave here in the moonlight, almost immediately if you want to live past dawn."

"How much do I tell the others?" Ian, who still hadn't made up his mind, asked.

"When you hand over these papers to Steve, show him this ring and bring it back to me here, go now."

Ian approached the second camp, handed over the papers and showed the ring to Steve. Whose face turned pale. He handed the papers to Ken and followed Ian back down to the creek via the horses as cover. Ian didn't know what to expect and was amazed to watch Steve and Barry hug each other in total silence.

"No names Steve," Barry requested.

"If I'm blessed with a son I'll name him after you, using your real Christian name," Steve said with deep emotion in his voice.

"Steve you must leave here now, make your camp look like men are asleep in it, crawl to your horses and go. Ian and Bill will go by doing the same after you've gone. Alex and I will leave later."

"You sense men coming here?"

"Yes Steve, I want you out of here in the next half an hour."

They embraced again and Barry watched Steve leave like a shadow in the night. Within a short time Barry watched the three men leave like shadows, riding down the valley amongst the trees, not even disturbing the wildlife.

"Is Hodge your real name?" Ian asked.

"No, Ian, so don't ask." He smiled and said, "Ask Charley to keep a close eye on Alex, they won't let him off lightly. Frank Black is equally guarded as is John Sefton. They are both leaders," adding, "Bill will be enormously curious, please keep my identity safe. If I'm killed, I'd like to be buried in the Hill Top cemetery, even then keep my secret. You can tell Bill that I worked for John Sefton only after I'm dead."

"He probably won't forgive me," Ian laughed and said in a soft voice.

"I think he will in time Ian. Good-bye."

Barry walked back to the camp he was sharing with Alex, who had just witnessed the others silently leaving like shadows in the night.

"Do you know what is going on Barry?" he asked.

"A message was received down near the creek, saying we all have to leave here now, but to leave the camp as if men are sleeping in it."

"Why wasn't I told?"

"I was down at the creek having a wash and said I'd tell you. We can crawl to our horses with our equipment in a couple of trips," Barry said with a grin, adding, "We ought to arrive at the camp, two hours above Hill Top, in early twilight tomorrow night."

Alex wasn't happy about being left out of serious discussions and planned to have a good talk to Ian when he next saw him, being in an irritated mood now.

Barry had to endure the rough side of Alex's tongue once the sun rose in the east. They rode at a steady pace all day, and it was a relief to arrive at their favourite campsite, beside a creek in early twilight. Even though it was only two hours from Hill Top, all the men liked the views and it was a good place to fish and relax. Usually after each camp the men would leave a pile of wood for the next campers, but not tonight, leaving only enough to get the fire going and put the quart-pots on the fire. It was never a good idea to leave the camp unattended, but this evening they had no choice. They both walked around the corner of the creek to collect more firewood.

To the east was a small group of trees, which was usually where the men went to relieve bodily functions. Both men were tired and ate a sparse meal, though Alex complained about a bitter taste in his tea. Barry didn't take a lot of notice because Alex hadn't improved his mood all day and was still irritable.

"Where are you going?" Alex asked as Barry stood up.

"To make myself feel comfortable before going to my swag."

"Don't be long."

There was an unusual tone to the words Alex had said and Barry wondered what was going on in his mind, perhaps he was trying to make amends after a bad day, but he didn't look well. Once in amongst the first line of trees, Barry began to undo some lower buttons, when he felt someone behind him, and was beginning to turn when he recognised the voice.

"No names Barry."

"What are you doing here at this time of the night?"

"Waiting for you Barry."

"You'd see me at the barracks in the morning."

"I don't think so."

"I wish you would explain yourself, I have to get back to Alex, he isn't well."

"He'll be lucky to survive the night."

"What's going on?"

"This night is all about you Barry, you have become surplus to our operation."

There was no warning, he saw the silver gleam of the knife blade in the moonlight. Instead of passing water, he passed blood, lots of it and in those last few seconds of life, he thought of his adopted parents and his little brother who loved his tin whistle. The last sound he heard was of a native boy playing on a tin whistle. He dropped to the ground and never felt the soil on his face as his turned slightly to catch a moonbeam. His killer looked down and saw a smile on Barry's face. He was beyond understanding and only thought how satisfying it was to kill such a useless life.

*

In the middle of the morning Sergeant Green was outside his office talking with Charley, Bill and Ian, when suddenly they heard a cry of help from the horse yard. The three men ran down to the yard, followed at a more seemly pace by the Sergeant. They were shocked to see Alex ride bareback into the yard, Charley grabbed him as he fell from his saddle to the ground

"Been drugged, something bitter in the tea, had to leave our camp to get wood, someone must have put it in my quart-pot, don't know where Barry is. He went to the first line of trees as usual and never came back to the camp," he said, slurring his words.

Seconds later he lost consciousness in front of his shocked friends. The Sergeant gave instant directions for Charley to come to his office. Alex was promptly conveyed to the nearest doctor.

Chapter 22

ergeant Green had to forget about Alex for the time being and concentrate on sending a man up to collect Barry, if he was in trouble. This matter had an unsettling feel about it; he could see that Charley was deeply distressed, but he was the best man for the job. He sent a message with the request that Charley was to come to his office please. Charley duly arrived and once seated in front of the Sergeant's, waited to hear his next job.

"I know you want to be with Alex Pitt, but he doesn't need you at the present time, that may well come later. I need you to go up to that camp and look for Barry and investigate the camp for any clues as to what has happened in that place."

"Do I take the dray and four horses?" Charley asked.

"Yes, you will need the dray to bring back a saddle if it's still at the camp."

"Who's to come with me?"

"Mr. Wade on his horse and Mr. Darkwood on the dray with you. The camp is only eight miles from here, so I'll expect you back tonight."

"And in case of difficulties?"

"Alright, take your swags and tell the other men."

"Yes Sergeant, I will."

He stood up and halfway out the doorway, turned as the man at the desk said quietly, "Don't worry about Mr. Pitt, he'll get the best of care."

Charley and Alex had trained together and were close friends, most of the time! Now he wanted to know who had harmed his friend, he remembered a Senior officer he had worked alongside in the city. This man had used clay to get a footprint for evidence. Charley decided to use this same method at the camp site, now he had use of the dray. He went to the cooking area and managed to borrow a large flat pan.

"Can I borrow the flat pan hanging from your saddle?" he asked Ian on his way back to the dray.

"What do you want to do with it, Charley?"

He explained and Ian enquired, "Won't one flat pan be enough for the job?"

"Not if we're under observation and want to get a sample back to here at the office."

"Right, I'll get it for you."

"Thank you Ian, will you also visit Alex when he wakes up and explain to him that I have to go on a job."

"I will Charley, Alex is special to us too, you do know that don't you?"

"I know, but he's like a brother, although sometimes an irritating one too!'

"Don't worry, he's in the best of hands and he'll survive whatever was put into his quart-pot."

"The F——- bastards,"

Charley saw Willie and called out, "Get your swag and put it on the dray, we're leaving for the campsite."

They drove away in a northerly direction. The benefit of four horses was that the journey could be achieved a lot faster than with only two horses, As Charley drove along he explained to his two colleagues about the use of clay. He had their instant attention to this plan and assured him they would be careful in where they put their boots. They knew the camp as they had frequently used it. Once the horses were hobbled and the single horse unsaddled, James called out loudly, "BARRY!"

Nothing disturbed the birds in the trees and only a silence greeted the call. James walked up to a group of trees where they'd all gone to relieve themselves at one time or another. He walked past the first line of trees and saw a pair of black boots lying on the grass. A bit further and the body of a policeman became visible. His first thought was how peaceful it was here amongst the trees, followed by the realization of murder and a cold shiver gave his body a shake.

"Charley come here," he called out loudly.

Willie followed and both men looked down at Barry for a couple of moments. No one moved until Charley spoke, "We have a little time before we have to take Barry back to Hill Top. I want clay prints of the boot marks in this soft soil, it appears Barry has fallen forward, I want the marks of the prints behind him."

"Do we take one of Barry's boots off him to check his prints?" Willie asked.

Charley gave a positive reply.

"What do you want me to do?" James asked.

"Find some clay and water, not too much in the pan and I'll do the rest of the job."

While James was away digging up clay, Charley sent Willie to find Barry's horse and bring it back to where the other horses were hobbled.

"Willie, see if you can find where other horses have stood on the far side of this group of trees. See if you recognise any of their hoof marks, for example the marks their iron shoes make, horses walk differently the same as we do and wear at different points," he also suggested.

The men were quite busy acting upon his requests, and soon clay was being put over prints on the soft soil. Behind the trees, Willie had found an interesting hoof mark, which he recognised as belonging to their police stables. Charley used Ian's flat pan for the hoof print. He actually set it in the pan and closed the lid after it had dried. This way it would stay in one piece until they returned to the barracks.

Charley couldn't see any different foot marks in the camp itself. Their main discovery concerned the boot marks, behind where Barry had been standing, were made by police footwear. There was no doubt in their minds, the prints were made by police boots. They managed to get a good set of prints, and after drying, were carefully put in the large pan. Such was their concentration no one noticed George Nash riding up to the camp until the last moment as they had been so engrossed in putting the clay prints in safely.

"Playing mud pies Charley, I can help you," George said looking down from his horse.

Without any warning he poured a container of water into the pan, then urged his horse forward, it's hooves upset the pan and the clay returned to the soil, leaving the pan empty.

"You're a right F— bastard George," Charley expressed their combined feelings.

"I told you I'd get even with you. I was told you were getting evidence of some kind, so I thought I'd spoil it for you," George laughed.

"Someone murdered Barry Hodge," Willie said.

"He won't be missed, now I won't have to pay him back all that money, I borrowed from him. It's an ill wind for him and a good one for me," George replied.

"We'll remember you George when we're passing around the hat for Barry's burial," James called out as he turned to ride away.

"You won't get a penny out of me."

"F– bastard, he'll cough up his share of the burial costs, if I have squeeze it out of him," Charley growled deep in his throat.

"You've seen how to do it, remember and improve on my methods if you can, don't ever give up on good ideas, you will always have the bastards in our job who will be difficult about new ideas." Charlie said as they watched George ride away .

No one wanted to stay the night near the dead body, but there was no choice in the matter, working all day with the clay. Barry was now wrapped up in his own swag in the dray which was parked a little way beyond where the horses were hobbled. It wasn't the happiest of camps and they turned in earlier than usual after the final mugs of tea. Needless to say they avoided the top side of the group of trees. There were loud curses when the men tripped over unexpected branches or logs in the darkness.

Before sun rise they set off for Hill Top, following a creek between two hills on a lovely morning, when suddenly masked men descended upon them, springing out of the undergrowth so there was no escape for James on his horse and leading another one. Normally even bad men respected the dead, but not these men. They pulled Barry's body from the dray, using an axe, which they had brought for the purpose of cutting off his head. They then kicked it at each man like a ball, while those on the horses laughed. Charley had put some of the broken clay back in the pan. One of the men saw it and said as he lent forward in his saddle and tipped it out.

"I've heard about this method from a city mate," he said.

He rode his horse over the broken clay pieces until they resembled clods of soil. Not another word was spoken to the police, who were surprised at their behaviour but not shocked, after all this was the frontier. The masked men at last kicked the now unrecognisable head, mounted their horses and rode back into the undergrowth. For a few moments Willie and Charley remained sitting on the dray, then Charley said, "Come on Willie me lad let's put Barry back together again."

"Like Humpty Dumpty had a great fall?" Willie laughed and said.

"'He was a cannon in the English Civil War and fell off a wall and couldn't be fixed. Barry isn't at all like him," Charley said.

"How do you know that Charley?"

They put Barry back in his swag and left the head to one side.

"My Mother told me, lots of those rhymes are political ditties of an earlier age."

They talked about their favourite rhymes the whole way back to Hill Top, it was better than being constantly aware of what the death of Barry meant to them, that his death was at the hand of a fellow colleague.

Back at Hill Top the body was left at the medical tent. Some men were engaged to dig a new grave in the newly designated area for the cemetery a little way out from the community. Barry would be buried before sunset. The news spread like wild fire that a policeman had been murdered. The community was shocked particularly when they heard how his head had been treated as a ball. At the same time no one was interested in going after the men who had committed this outrage. After all a dead head is already dead, they all had live ones!

Sergeant Green asked Ian and Bill to go out on a job for a couple of days.

"Mr. Todd be kind enough to prepare both saddles and rations for Mr. Percy and yourself, Mr. Percy is preparing a report for me at this moment, " he said.

Bill was quite happy to complete this job. Not being able to find Ian's flat pan attached to his saddle, where it usually was kept, he went looking for it and was surprised to find it beside Charley's saddle. Bill was surprised to find it full of clay, he cleaned it out and put it back on the saddle.

After making the report, Ian wandered down to the stables and saw the pan now attached to his saddle.

"Had Charley finished with it?" he asked.

"I don't know, I found it full of clay and washed it out. What was he doing with it?" Bill enquired.

"How soon can you be ready to ride Bill?" Ian asked.

"What's the hurry Ian?"

"Charley will be furious with you. You and Charley can't stand each other and this will be worse than usual."

"What will be?"

"My flat pan had the clay print of the horse who had been ridden from our stables. It's believed the man who rode the horse, is a policeman who killed Barry. What was in my pan was the evidence."

"How was I to know, no one has told me anything about clay prints, I've never heard of such a method. So that's what Charley has been doing?"

"Yes, it is something he saw done in the city."

"I'll get my saddle bag Ian and we'll leave now."

Bill was no coward and went to find him, standing at a distance he addressed him, "I didn't know about your clay print. I was asked to prepare for a patrol, found the flat pan full of clay and cleaned it out, before returning it to Ian's saddle."

Charley's face changed colour and he spoke quietly, "I suppose it had to be you. Well I hope you like having an unknown murderer sleeping in your barracks."

Charley sighed and turning walked away. Bill watched him leave, more in surprise than any other emotion. Charley not throwing a tantrum was a new experience for Bill, which somehow made it worse. He returned to Ian and mounted their horses and rode out of the yard,

"I'm going to look after Alex in the community medical tent. I hope we can go home when he is better," Charley spoke to Willie.

"We don't want you to return to the city Charley, or Alex, so just get him better first and then we might talk about it," Willie replied quietly.

"You need a haircut boy," Charley said, ruffling Willie's hair, before walking out the gate on his way to the medical tent.

In the office the Sergeant carefully examined Barry's saddle and after a while found the hidden pouch, cleverly disguised. He smiled as he withdrew a paper, which told that he knew he'd been betrayed by a member of the barracks police. He'd been heard talking to Ian Percy late one night recently. Barry had also written that he thought George Nash wasn't involved in the operation in any way. He was a gamester, who frequently lost money which made him sour. Barry had also written, 'I'm also sure you have two men in deep cover in your barracks, one is a killer, so be careful. I don't know who they are yet, I have my suspicions. I will tell a friend who will inform you if I'm unable to do so in person.'

The Sergeant put the paper down and wondered what the clay print would reveal, as they now had nothing else. He was pleased George Nash would be leaving in a couple of days' time, he'd been given the required number of months' notice. Three new policemen were being sent from the city.

Ian and Bill hadn't gone far when Ian said, "I think we ought to return to make sure the Sergeant knows about your error, with my pan."

They rode back and tied their horses to the hitching rail, close to the office.

"I thought you two would have been miles away from here by now," Sergeant Geen said looking up in surprise.

Ian then explained why they had returned. The sergeant showed none of his obvious disappointment on hearing Ian's and Bill's words.

"How would anyone know Mr. Todd. When you return Mr. Nash will have resigned and left Hill Top," he said quietly.

"I've been told he's going to the southern gold fields with the gaming tent," Ian said.

"He told me that was his intention," the Sergeant replied.

"Perhaps the barracks will settle down now he had gone?" Ian commented.

"Barry Hodge is sure we have a killer and another man in deep cover, who is on the other side of our operation, in the barracks at the present time," the Sergeant spoke quietly. "Mr. Todd, the man you knew as Barry Hodge had special duties," he added.

"Do we know where we all were on the night Barry Hodge was murdered?" Ian asked.

The Sergeant sat very still and replied slowly, "That's a difficult question Mr. Percy. I know where I've sent men to do general duties but I'm not entirely sure of their other activities in the time in which Barry had his throat cut."

"What did Charley think about the time of his death?"

"Mr. Rush was of the opinion that he was killed in mid-twilight. He based these words on the fact that men don't go up to the trees when they can't see the ground, not wishing to stand on a snake."

Bill hid his smile, knowing full well it wasn't a snake they didn't want to stand upon, it was other leavings of other men. He must have made a tiny sound, because Ian kicked him on the shin.

"Did Charley have any other ideas?" Ian asked.

"He said very little wood had been burnt, he thought Mr. Pitt may have passed out, as Barry was walking up to the trees. Mr. Rush is absolutely sure the killer is one of our men, they tested their boots with the foot prints. None of them have any doubt about the police boot marks."

"The hoof print?" Ian asked.

"The farrier can't remember, in the last two days he has replaced several iron shoes. He can't remember which horse the shoes were attached to, he found one with the small indenture on one side of the shoe, which Mr. Rush identified. Unfortunately the farrier can't remember which horse he had replaced it."

"Which men were here in the barracks on that night?" Ian enquired.

The Sergeant peered at a list he'd made yesterday afternoon and replied, "Mr. Hale arrived late in the afternoon from Sunny Flat, he'd taken a second warning down to Tom Hunt. Mr. Nash had been sent to warn a drover not to steal stock from other squatters on his way north. He arrived back here in early twilight. Mr. Wade had been sent out to a new settlement called Duck's Creek, to warn the general store owner that raiders were operating in his area and to be careful, he returned in the early evening. Mr. Stokes was in the barracks, having arrived in the late afternoon. Mr. Sharp arrived from the south, well after dark, he'd made a delivery to a squatter. Lastly Mr. Darkwood." The Sergeant smiled and explained, "The squatter in question always asks for him in particular, he has two daughters who are of marriageable age. He has his eye firmly set on Mr. Darkwood and invents reasons to ask for him."

"How does Willie manage this plan, with all the work he has to do?" They laughed and Ian asked .

"This has been going on for a few weeks and I rather think Mr. Darkwood has been enjoying the exploration of a certain attractive young lady. They give him lots of mugs of ale. On the way back here he chews a particular leaf, in the hope I won't know. It is a dead giveaway!!" adding, "I warned him to be careful, as you know Mr. Darkwood sometimes expresses words best left unsaid." The Sergeant laughed at this memory and continued, "He spoke quite frankly and I had to keep a straight face until he left my office. Mr. Darkwood said cheerfully 'I'm not worried, she's bedding two men, sons of squatters around her father's farm. She'll marry one of them and will probably never know who's the father of her child between the three of us!'"

"One day some girl will be fortunate to catch Willie," Bill looked surprised and commented.

"I agree with you, he's a good man. As he gets older he's the kind of policeman we want in these remote areas, between the old world and the new one developing," the Sergeant continued.

Ian looked down at the rough boards at his feet, then up to meet the eyes of his Sergeant, and asked, "How was the murder committed by one of our own men?"

"Perhaps someone wore police boots to put us off the scent. The obvious choice would be Mr. Sharp, but I've had it confirmed he did go south, and it was a long way back to our barracks."

"If it was Bernie Sharp, he won't see old bones. He's a loose screw and I wouldn't like him keeping any of my secrets," Ian mused quietly.

"What game do you think the opposition is playing Mr. Percy?"

Ian remained silent as he considered the Sergeant's question, before speaking slowly, "I think they are ramping up problems for us to solve, which will keep us away from the real problem, which is protecting the Sefton family, and working towards the arrest of Frank Black."

Chapter 23

His Sergeant smiled a knowing expression and asked gently, "Mr. Percy, I think you saw Mr. Baker and Mr. Hodge meet. Tell me what you saw please.?"

Ian's face showed surprise and not a little discomfort as he turned to his friend Bill and said, "Bill I was asked to give my word that I wouldn't reveal what I saw that night in early twilight, but now our world has changed with Barry's murder." Before Ian could stop himself he asked, "How did you know Sergeant? I'm sorry, not thinking straight," he said instantly.

"As with Mr. Todd, a little bird sang a tune and I heard it. Now I want your impression please Mr. Percy" His Sergeant smiled and replied taking the possible sting out of his words.

"Barry Hodge played a dangerous game and until the night in question I had a poor opinion of him, considering him a foolish type of man. In a split second I was shocked to witness his meeting with Steve Baker, a man whom I have considerable respect for. They greeted each other like cousins and I suddenly realised I'd been hoodwinked into thinking he was a fool, because that's what he wanted me to think." After a few moments Ian continued, "I've always prided myself on my ability to assess other men but in Barry I failed miserably, I don't know who he was, or even if Barry Hodge was his real name?"

There was a long silence before the Sergeant spoke gently, "We were all at fault with Barry Hodge. I value your assessment of the present situation and I agree with you, it is getting more dangerous as the weeks roll on. I'm sending you both down to "Red's Land" to tell them about the murder. You'll very likely find out a lot more about Barry Hodge. I ask that what you hear, you keep secret. Your word gentlemen?"

Both Ian and Bill gave their word of honour to keep silent. Both men were accustomed to keeping secrets, sometimes even from each other, but perhaps not for long. Before continuing their journey, Ian went to the stables to ask a question of the farrier.

"It was my free night with my family, the stables were unattended until the morning."

*

On the night when the farrier was absent, a man left the barracks quietly and walked east to the edge of the police paddock, climbed over the wooden fence to where his horse stood, saddled and tied it to a tree. He mounted and rode for a couple of hours to a meeting place, above a squatter's hut on a hill, where a small fire was burning, which made it easy to see as he approached from the west. He didn't have long to wait, until another man rode up to the fire and dismounted and knelt down to warm his hands,

"Has the job been completed?" he looked up and asked.

"Yes, and Alex Pitt is out too, he'll be lucky to wake up."

"Good."

"Where is the man who made a trip for us?"

"He has stopped breathing. Once your spare uniform has been washed it will be returned to you."

"Why did you kill him, we could've used him again?"

"We don't want loose ends, this is a warning for you too, don't ask dangerous questions."

"Where are you going now?"

The other man glared at the younger man and said in a brittle voice, "I've warned you and I won't warn you again, use my name and you will die."

The younger man left the fire, mounted his horse and rode back to his barracks.

If he had looked back at the hill, he would have seen another horseman arrive, and dismount and walk to the fire. He looked into the flames as he stirred the coals, watching the swirl of sparks rise into the sky.

"Is Barry Hodge out of the way?" he asked.

"Well and truly."

"Good. At a suitable time deal with the other loose end."

"The man who dealt with Hodge?"

"Yes, we don't need him anymore," he said before mounting his horse and riding away.

The first man did the same and rode back down the hill to meet up with a third man. Details were passed on and he rode back to the police barracks at the settlement of Hill Top. He arrived after midnight and saw the other man in his bunk asleep.

Chapter 24

Bill was quiet as he rode out of the police yard behind Ian on this short patrol. He wasn't happy with his friend for keeping the secret about that idiot Barry Hodge, who now seemed to be different from the man they had known in the barracks. Ian was aware of Bill's feelings and wondered how he could approach the problem without making it worse. The answer came in a flash.

"When were you going to tell me about your latest girl you've been visiting at night?" Ian asked waiting until Bill rode up beside him.

Bill nearly fell out of his saddle in shock, and in a sudden movement pulled on his reins, causing his horse to take exception to an uncalled-for jab on its mouth. It took Bill a couple of minutes to settle his horse down again. Ian watched with interest, waiting for his friend to give an answer or at least an attempt to do so.

"You needn't look so pleased about it," Bill said, not in the least amused.

"I didn't say a word Bill"

"You didn't have to say a F— word."

They rode for another couple of miles before Ian asked, "Well Bill, do you want to talk about her?"

"No I don't want to talk about her, you know damn well I won't talk about her. You don't have to talk about Barry Hodge either."

"Fair is fair Bill."

"You can be irritating at times Ian."

"We both can be, that's why we get on together so well, most of the time."

They rode in silence until Bill asked, "What's the job we have to do before going down to 'Red's Land', the Sergeant spoke quietly about it?"

"It's tied up with the operation and the little birds which talk to him. There's a squatter with land east of our barracks and he has some information which our Sergeant wants to know. We are to get it and return to Hill Top. He'll have more rations for us, and then we'll ride south."

"Does that mean it will probably be twilight when we make the delivery to him?"

"Yes, but not at our barracks, we're to meet him on the edge of the community. He told me that he'll send Willie ahead to make a camp for us down the track."

"How will he know?"

"I suppose the moment we're seen, he'll send Willie to the chosen site."

They rode on towards the meeting place, not at his hut, but at a camp on the edge of his land. It was a place well known to the police, as they camped there on a frequent basis when working in this area. The camp was on a rise near available water and it had been suggested that they arrive at dusk and he would come a bit later to avoid being seen by any passing men.

"It sounds as if he's afraid of something?" Bill said thoughtfully.

"I think anyone who passes messages to our Sergeant, has very good reasons to be very careful indeed."

"Does this man have a name?"

"Yes, his name is William Carter and he's helpful to the police."

"I haven't heard that name before today."

"That's because he was known for a long time by another name, which we have conveniently forgotten, now he's changed his way of life," Ian laughed and replied before adding a name.

"Now I know him! I arrested him once a long time ago in my first year, I liked him and I seem to remember he had a pretty wife," Bill said laughing.

"Remember Bill you are seeing a pretty girl so don't look at her!"

"I will be quite correct with William."

They met up with him, and enjoyed his company beside the fire, and the meat he'd brought for the last meal of the day. William was a good-looking man, tall and well-built, brown hair and beard carefully trimmed. Ian noticed he was wearing clean clothes and looked respectable.

"A few days ago I saw three policemen on horses, one of the men I knew wasn't a policeman," William delivered his information after general conversation.

"How did you know he wasn't a policeman?" Bill asked.

"I'd employed him three months ago, he was a bad man and I had to dismiss him."

"What did he do?" Ian asked.

"He was disrespectful to my wife in a way I couldn't overlook."

"I take it he tried to rape her?" Bill said.

"Yes, he's fortunate to be still alive.'

"What was he doing that made you want to contact us William?" Ian enquired.

"He's the image of one of your younger mounted policemen, in your uniform no one would know he wasn't a real policeman."

He stopped talking as he saw the unguarded expressions on the faces of Bill and Ian, his information was vital to their work. They stayed the night and when they awoke before the rising of the sun, William had already left, as silently as he'd arrived the night before.

Ian and Bill had an uneventful ride back to the edge of the Hill Top community in early twilight, meeting their Sergeant on the southern approach to the settlement. As previously arranged Willie rode forth as soon as they were sighted on the track. They rode up beside their Sergeant's horse and passed on the information.

"Mr. Darkwood has your added rations. Thank you for s job well done," he said.

They watched their Sergeant ride back in the direction of the barracks, before turning and riding southwards, until in the distance they saw the light of a fire.

At last they rode up to the prepared camp in the moonlight, situated near a waterhole, to see hot coals waiting for slabs of meat to be put on the fire. The only job they were required to do was to hobble their horses, after unsaddling them and checking their welfare for the night.

Willie had made a good camp, enjoying the peace and quiet after being in the barracks for the last few nights. He was still upset that Charley had lost all his evidence, and refrained from making any comments to Bill, though he did manage to ask him, "What's it like growing old?"

Ian smiled as he waited to hear Bill's response.

"I don't know Willie, not yet being old, as my girlfriend keeps telling me. She says I'm better than younger men she knows of about your age Willie!"

Ian smiled, his friend was holding his own against his mischievous colleague.

"I suppose she doesn't want to lose you, being at that time of life!" Willie continued.

Ian decided to step in before this conversation got out of hand.

"Willie, will you be so kind as to check our horses please?" he suggested.

"Yes Ian, I'm only too pleased to go and check your mounts, after all they've had a heavy load of years to carry all day!"

He skipped out of the camp before either man could get hold of him, laughing as he vanished amongst the trees. One horse had wandered away with a broken hobble, so by the time he returned to the camp, having mended the hobble, both men were asleep in their swags.

In the morning Willie left his swag and prepared the fire, knowing these men liked their tea before any other food.

'The aging ones are waking up at last!" he said under his breath as he settled the quart-pots on the coals.

Bill took one look at his expression and had a fair idea what was in his mind, as long as he didn't say it!

Willie cooked most of the meat and said as they saddled their horses, "You can chew on cooked meat as you ride along, I didn't cook it too much, so it will be soft enough for you!"

Bill ground his teeth at the word 'soft' as Ian hid a smile and replied, "Thanks Willie."

They rode south in the half light of the early morning, and with no sign of the sun, it was just light in the eastern sky.

"He couldn't help himself, even at breakfast," Bill commented, some hours later.

"He's young and under considerable pressure in the barracks, laughter is a way of dealing with it, Bill."

They talked as they rode across a known landscape.

Chapter 24

Three weeks earlier, before Ian and Bill rode down to 'Red's Land', Alan Gill was standing outside his house at 'River Oaks' watching three men approach on horses. He called to his wife, Eva and even from a distance she recognised Frank Black.

"What do you think he wants with us?" she said.

"I don't know Eva."

"Is our past going to be resurrected and haunt us in our new life?"

"Perhaps?"

"Be polite to him Alan, no matter how he behaves to us. We have our children to protect, not just ourselves."

"Don't worry Eva, I'm not about to give up all we've achieved here on this land."

"Do you mean we will have to play whatever game he is here to sell us?"

"If it's the price for staying here, then yes as you said we have our children's welfare to fight for now. Warn the girls to be very careful and I'd suggest you go inside and make tea. We'll have it on the verandah, behave naturally, don't give him an edge to be nasty."

Eva retreated into the house and seeing her daughters said, "We're about to have some visitors, I want you to ride out to where Victor is working with the cattle. Send him home and you take over his work please."

"Who is it Mum?" Betty enquired.

"Not a good man, he's called Inspector Frank Black."

"What does he want with us Mum?"

"Betty, please leave now."

Eva was clearly upset and her daughters, who had never known the urgency to hurry, were slow to get ready to leave the house. They'd been so secure at "River Oaks." Betty opened the back door to be confronted by an unknown man who pushed her back inside the door. g

"Get back in there, you're going nowhere today," he said.

He had a gun in his hand and they retreated back inside the house. Anne burst into tears, Betty was also shocked but she now exhibited an iron calm, inherited from a distant ancestor who had faced down armed bandits.

"Go to your room until I return, no arguments, go." Eva told Anne.

Betty went to Victor's room and took a pair of his trousers and a shirt and changed into them while stuffing her hair under one of his hats.

Her Mother came to the doorway, "Be careful Betty, these are dangerous men, tell Victor to come into the house through your window and he's not to be seen," she said.

Eva watched her daughter climb through the window and vanish behind some bushes and breathed a sigh of relief as she saw her ride down to the creek, well undercover from anyone watching the house.

Eva made tea, put cakes on a tray and had it ready to go out on to the verandah, but first she went to Anne's room.

"Stay here please Anne," she said.

"Where is Betty?"

"She's gone to get Victor."

"But why?"

"We're in danger Anne."

"Tell me, why are we in danger when I can see a policeman on our front verandah?"

"Not this man, he isn't like our other police friends. This man is called Inspector Frank Black and he's very dangerous."

"You saw the man at the back door?" Eva said, knowing her time was short.

"Yes Mum."

"He's a policeman," adding with a silent wish, "Anne please don't do anything which could get us all shot."

Her Mother left the room and closed the door. Anne wasn't accustomed to having anyone speak to her in such a commanding manner and was inclined to be resentful of the fact. She hadn't experienced hardship in her short life and had no comprehension of the power of the man who was sitting on the front verandah, playing a game with a frightened man, her father.

The Inspector liked what he had seen of 'River Oaks' and in his own way was pleased to see that Alan and Eva had done well for themselves. His humour increased knowing they wouldn't want to lose it all now.

"No one is to leave the house." he said as he dismounted and instructed his two men.

"What if they do?"

"A bullet ought to be warning enough."

"Right Inspector Black."

As he tied his reins to the hitching rail, he thought the children of convicts were open season, a word from him in the right place and the Gills could find themselves in a road gang or at least being turned off 'River Oaks'. He'd done it before to un-cooperative couples with children. Now it was the Gill's time to co-operate and he smiled as he walked forward to greet Alan Gill.

Alan saw that smile on the Inspector's face and gave a silent shiver, as he knew a good deal about the methods employed by Inspector Black, from his late father. Alan was a good actor, he had taught himself from a young age to be confident and never show his insecurities.

As he stepped off his verandah there was no trace of his inner feelings visible on his face. The approaching Inspector suffered a moment or two of shock, this was not how victims were expected to behave, then he smiled remembering he had the upper hand. Deep in Alan's mind, he thought he had a wolf on his land and in his own space with his family.

"Good morning Inspector Black what a pleasant surprise,": he greeted his visitor.

"Hello Alan, I see you've done well for yourself on this land."

"Yes Inspector, the cattle prices have been good. To what do we owe the visit of yourself on this sunny morning?'

"I was passing your gate, when I thought of you and the up-coming marriage of your daughter Anne, is it?"

"That's correct, she's to marry a fine young man called Roy Cook."

Eva arrived on the verandah with tea and cakes, in time to hear her husband's words and she greeted the Inspector cautiously, which he duly noted with a smile. She sat down and poured the tea into mugs, keeping a subdued position and showing no emotion. She had known Frank Black for many years as he had lived near her parents' house. He'd been a cruel boy and had become even worse as a policeman. Eva had an inner strength and an iron will, which she was able to hide in a show of weakness.

"Are you aware of Roy Cook's Mother's occupation?" Inspector Black asked.

"She is a woman in the city," Alan replied.

"That's true enough, but she's a prostitute and Cook could be anyone?" The Inspector laughed and said.

"No, she couldn't be," Eva exclaimed, showing instant shock.

The cold black eyes laughed at her dismay, as his lips replied, "Yes Eva, a woman of the streets. What will it be like having her in your house, wondering if your visiting men had known her in other ways, only another girl of the streets would know. He added, "I've come here out of the kindness of my heart."

I'm sure if he ever had a heart, he lost it years ago, Eva thought.

"What are we to do Inspector Black?" Alan asked.

"I hear you have in your care the land Titles of a block of land just north of your land, in Roy Cook's name. Is that correct?"

Yes, that's correct."

"I have in my saddlebag a new set of papers made out in your name, for a price. I want to see those papers made in Roy Cook's name burnt. You can buy the land from the state, the details of which I will deliver to the right authorities," adding, "You don't want an unsuitable owner on your northern boundary do you?"

Alan thought this is the crux of the Inspector's visit, Roy's land.

Unknown to those on the verandah, Victor had followed Betty through her window and went to Anne's room, while Betty dressed into her own clothes. The three of them walked quietly into the front room and listened to the conversation outside the window. The menace in the Inspector's voice was evident, and Victor and Betty gave their attention to Anne, when she heard she couldn't marry Roy. They could only make signs to her to keep silent.

"We are in great danger, if he finds out we've been listening," Victor whispered.

Anne seemed to understand and Betty thought she didn't comprehend what the Titles meant for herself and Roy. They heard their Father go inside to his desk and retrieve the papers Roy had entrusted to his care. He handed them to the Inspector, who glanced at them and said, "They're all here."

A few minutes later the papers burning and turning to ash on the ground below the steps where Eva was sitting. She saw his satisfied smile, as he now handed a note to Alan saying, "You owe me that sum."

"Right now?"

"Yes, I believe you have it from your recent sale of cattle."

Alan paid the required sum, it was cheap at the price to get rid of this visitor. Inside, Betty turned to see that Anne had disappeared.

"Where has Anne gone?" She said urgently to Victor.

"I'll go out to the verandah and you look out of the windows," Victor replied.

Anne was aware of the danger that her family was experiencing, she had remembered Roy telling her about this Inspector. She knew she couldn't possibly face those three men, she sensed a real darkness in them. As she listened to the talk, a smile crossed her lips and a thought grew in her mind. As Victor and Betty were intent on what was being said outside the window, she quietly left the room and taking a sharp knife, left the house. The hitching rail was out of sight of the verandah and the two men were not in sight. Anne knew exactly what to do to create a problem miles from 'River Oaks'. She was back in the house before Betty found her in the kitchen shed behind the main house, putting the knife away in a drawer.

"Where have you been Anne?" Betty asked.

"Out in the fresh air, Betty."

On the front verandah Victor was introduced to the Inspector, who enquired, "Where have you been this morning?"

"Out working with our cattle."

The Inspector turned to one of his men and gave a nasty expression, and turning back to Victor asked, "Do you normally come home at this time of the day?"

"Yes Inspector, I forgot my saddlebag."

"Stupid boy." Victor smiled at the insult, as the Inspector continued, "Your Father has just bought Roy's Grant of land, what do you think about that land now?"

"We run our cattle on it Inspector, so I don't suppose we'll have remove them any time in the future."

"Cold boy aren't you?"

"Life is life Inspector."

"Your father deserves you boy," grunting a farewell and left taking his men with him.

"Do you think we've seen the last of him Alan?" Eva asked.

"I certainly hope so, a nasty piece of work."

Eva remained seated and stated in front of all her family, "Red Bryant has asked for all the cattle we can spare for a secret operation, we'll assist him when he calls for our help. I trust Red Bryant."

Alan had listened and replied, "Eva we can't do it."

She gave Alan a look which he recognised and accepted with resignation, as she stated again, "Alan we will do it, the matter is now closed for discussion. Victor, you will ride up to 'Red's Land' and inform Red of our decision."

"Do I tell what happened here today?" He turned to his Father and asked.

"Yes Victor, we had no choice in the matter."

Eva heard from Betty that Anne had been missing for some time, she'd found her in the kitchen putting a knife away in a drawer but Anne wouldn't reveal what she'd been doing with the knife. A couple of weeks later when Eva was visiting a neighbour, a day's ride from 'River Oaks', she'd been told, "We had an unexpected visit from an Inspector of Police, he wasn't a nice man."

"Who was he Janet?"

"Inspector Black, he fell from his horse. He was riding fast over stoney ground, his girth strap broke and he had a nasty fall."

"Did he do much damage to himself, Janet?"

"Can't say too much, we had to promise to keep silent, he will need a stick for months."

"How do you think it happened Janet?"

His men told him it just broke, but Guy looked at it one night and told me it had been cleverly cut with a sharp knife."

"If you talk?" Eva enquired quietly.

"We lose our land."

"Not a word will I ever speak while that man is alive, Janet."

Eva smiled and thought 'one day I will tell my family, but only after I'm sure he is dead.' She had enjoyed her visit very much indeed.

Chapter 25

Bill and Ian hadn't been to 'Red's Land' for some time and the change from slab huts and leaking strips of bark on the roof, to brick and a shingle roof, was most welcome. Bill remembered trying to avoid an irritating drip while sitting at Red's table. They arrived in early twilight and only had time to see to the welfare of their horses, assisted by Kevin, get washed and generally cleaned up, before joining Red, his wife Mary and the other men, Roy, Steve, Ken and Jamie.

They hadn't any time before the meal to speak to Steve, when Red asked, "Why have you two gentlemen come down to visit us?"

"We've been sent down here to inform you that one of our colleagues has been murdered," Ian had no choice but to answer.

"Which one Ian?" Steve asked.

"Your cousin, Barry Hodge."

In the stunned silence, Roy took a tin whistle out of his pocket and played a tune on it. Bill, in shock, remembered Barry's words about his younger brother and the tin whistle and said, "Not cousin Ian, brother. You remember what he said to that little native boy, about his little brother having his best tin whistle. He gave his other one to the boy," he said breaking the silence.

Ian didn't show the shock he was feeling, listening to Bill's words.

"I do remember the sound of the tin whistle as it vanished into the undergrowth. This was an aspect we'd never seen in Barry before that morning," he said.

"Did he suffer?" Red asked.

"We don't think so, he knew his killer and his death was one slice of a knife across his throat," Bill replied.

"How do you know he knew the man who killed him?" Steve enquired.

"Charley Rush took clay prints from the soft soil, he was very sure the man wore police boots," Ian replied.

"Who'll ride and tell his widow, Harriet and his two boys, Donald and Gilbert?" Roy asked putting the tin whistle back in his pocket.

"I'll ride and tell her, the farm isn't too far from here," Ken said. He looked at Steve and added, "Will you ride and tell your Mother?"

"Yes, after I learn all the details." Steve looked at Bill and enquired, "Would you like to come with me Bill?"

"Roy?" Bill looked at Roy with a question.

"No Bill, not yet. I'll go later and see them. Our new Father doesn't know Barry was his eldest son, we are a family of secrets."

"Are you sure Roy?" Steve asked.

"Yes Steve, I asked Mother when I last saw her and she said it was best that he didn't know at the time."

"Does that mean he doesn't know he's a grandfather?"

"No, not yet."

"What name does Harriet live under?" Jamie enquired.

"Hodge for safety, but she knows it's Sefton," Roy informed him.

Mary Bryant had been listening to the conversation and said, "I've decided to go with you Ken, you can be my escort."

"Don't I get a say in this trip?" Red interjected.

"I've just told you Red, I don't think there's any more to say on the subject," his wife replied.

"Oh alright, have it your own way Mary," he said.

"I intend to Red."

The interested men wisely kept quiet as Red and his wife dealt with this matter, but silently they put their money on Mary, as they ate the excellent stew with vegetables and slices of damper to soak up the delicious gravy.

"Where does Harriet live?" Ian asked after he had finished eating.

"Harriet has a small slab house beside a school in a farming community, west of her brother Julian Webb's farm. She teaches the children of the local farmers," she replied.

"I'd like to go with you," Ian suggested.

"I'll be pleased if you would go with them Ian, then I'd be sure of Mary's safety," Red answered before his wife could even open her mouth.

Ken added words of encouragement to Mary, who said, "Now this matter has been dealt with in a satisfactory manner, who would like a helping of apple pie?"

A chorus greeted her words, Though the death of Barry had created an atmosphere of gloom over the table, general conversation flowed.

"Ken you can prepare Mary's horse in the morning, or do you want the dray Mary?" Red asked before they left the house for the night.

"No, I'll ride my horse, thank you Ken."

"When do you want to leave?" Red was pleased that Mary would be riding and asked.

"Before sunrise will be early enough, if it suits you Ken?"

"That's our usual time to go out of the camp."

"When will it suite you and Bill to leave here ?" Red looked at Steve and asked.

"The day after tomorrow."

As Bill and Ian walked across the open space to their hut near the stables, the night air was rent by the pure sound of a tin whistle, somewhere out in the moonlight. A mournful sound with an eerie quality attached to it and Bill felt a cold shiver pass down his spine.

"Roy playing that tin whistle is like that Old Man, like spirit talking to spirit," Bill commented.

"That's a deep thought for you Bill."

"Let's change the subject Ian, why do you want to go and see the widow?"

"I'd like to know what kind of girl Barry had married?"

"Not checking out the landscape by any chance?" Bill grinned and asked.

They laughed and entered the hut for the night.

Mary arrived at the stables dressed in clothes suitable for half a day's ride.

"Not a side saddle or a riding habit?" Ian said cheerfully.

"No Ian, not in my world with Red!"

She insisted in taking things for Harriet, which overflowed from her saddle bag into those of her escort, to their amusement. It was soon quite obvious that Mary was at home on her brown mare. She was happy to talk to the men on all kinds of subjects and they in turn were careful of the subject matter. Near 'Green Valley' Mary called a halt, dismounted from her horse saying, "Time for tea, Ken please make a fire."

"I'm here to identify each of you to Harriet. Without this introduction she'd never talk to you on the level she and Barry communicated about the operation," Mary explained after they'd eaten the food she had brought with her.

Chapter 26

"**A**re you saying Barry kept his wife informed of his work?" Ken enquired.

"Yes, and sent private papers into her safe keeping, this was in preparation for the time when he might not be able to visit her, like now."

"We're carrying the news of his death and at the same time, requesting her to talk about his work. Is she the kind of woman who can operate on this level?" Ian asked.

"Harriet could cope with anything at anytime, she and Barry have lived under the axe for the last three years. She had an unpleasant encounter with Frank Black and had to go into hiding," Mary replied.

"What happened to her?" Ken asked.

"She responded violently when he tried to take something from her against her will. Barry had taught her a few ways to protect herself. She kneed him you know where as hard as she could, after pulling her dress to rights. On his way to the floor, she slapped his face in fury, in response to his act as he had torn her blouse," Mary sighed and explained gently.

"What happened later?"

"His revenge was swift, with a death contract and then burnt down their house. They escaped with only the clothes they were wearing at the time. Friends assisted them to leave the city secretly and Barry brought Harriet to her brother. He established her away from 'Green Valley' in case he was investigated by Frank Black. She is quite safe as a school teacher."

"Where are we going today?" Ian enquired.

"To the school house via 'Green Valley' just so Jullian will know who we represent, otherwise he may call for re-enforcements."

They had a brief stop at the house of Jullian Webb and continued for another two hours. The school house was in the midst of small farms, giving it a good ring of protection. It was constructed of slab huts and accommodated for lots of children.

Ian didn't know what he was expecting after hearing about Harriet from Mary, but certainly not the vision of a slight woman in her mid-twenties with twinkling brown eyes, which he felt were reading his mind. He felt slightly ill at ease at being summed up even before an introduction. Harriet greeted Mary warmly who presented her with bulging saddlebags. Ken carried them into her house, which though seemingly small had several rooms. Outside was the school room on the other side of the cooking hut. Soon after they had arrived several men came to check that all was well with the teacher.

Mary took Harriet for a walk and told her about the death of her husband. She had an emotional hour with Mary and reluctantly returned to face the police, as she would've preferred more time with Mary. She would be able to mourn later in private with her children. Harriet sat on a log outside in the shade, there were tear marks on her face and began to speak quietly.

"We have lived under this threat for a long time, in a way it's a relief that it's all over. Lionel and I haven't been able to live together for three years and this aspect of marriage has been difficult for both of us. He always kept me informed of his activities and I have all his letters."

She stopped talking for a moment, to wipe away tears, and continued, "In his last communication he wrote that he didn't think he'd survive much longer. Most of that letter was personal. On a separate piece of paper he wrote some words and asked me to give the paper to anyone who came from the police, if he had been killed."

She handed the paper to Ian, who read it in shock, and gave it to Ken whose face turned pale.

"We'll have to leave early in the morning, to get an urgent message to Sergeant Green," he said quietly.

"But it's only a suspicion," Harriet said.

"Harriet, this man has been involved with the Hill Top police since the attack on the closed valley. He's responsible for the security of the barracks. I'm prepared to trust Barry's judgement," Ken answered.

"I see why you have to act. I found, over the years, that Lionel had a gift at seeing into a problem and making the right assessment. Sadly you will have to find the proof, at what cost, who is to know?" She smiled sadly and replied.

"Word must be sent to John Sefton," Ian added.

"When we get back to 'Red's Land' Jamie can ride to get that message to him," Ken spoke quietly.

They had a good night with some of the closer farming families coming to share the final meal of the day with their teacher and her visitors. It was quite obvious Harriet was deeply appreciated and guarded, as Ian discovered, much to his amusement. He decided it wouldn't be long before she nabbed herself a husband from among the local farmers. They rode back to 'Red's Land' and arrived late the next day. Within half an hour of their arrival, Jamie Tyson was on a horse and riding towards the ranges.

Chapter 27

Mary, with Ken and Ian, left early in the morning. After the normal jobs had been completed, Red, Roy, Steve and Jamie requested the full details of Barry's murder. This also included Bill's opinion as to the welfare of the Hill Top police. They had just sat down to lunch when Victor Gill arrived. It wasn't possible for Victor to talk to Roy privately before the meal. He had no option but to reveal the full extent of what had happened at 'River Oaks' during the visit of Inspector Frank Black.

"Is there going to be a wedding?" Red asked.

"I don't know. Mum and Dad are not happy."

"Did Anne say anything?" Roy asked quietly.

"She doesn't know, Roy"

"I wouldn't like to bet a lot of money on it Victor!" Roy replied.

"What does Betty think about us?" Steve enquired.

"I have no idea what any of us thinks about the aftermath of that visit. Please understand our parents have just told us that Inspector Black threatened to take 'River Oaks' from us because Dad's parents were convicts," A desperate note was clearly heard in Victor's voice as he answered Steve.

"Mine too," Bill said, adding, "The children of convicts are vulnerable to blackmail or worse, depending upon what is required for them to do or give up."

"Victor, tell your parents when this present problem is over our parents will pay a visit in the company of Red Bryant," Steve suggested.

"So I'm going down to 'River Oaks' am I?" Red laughed.

"Yes Red, with our parents to put the Gill family minds at rest on our Mother's occupation or lack of it."

"I'm happy to assist you Steve, and Roy," Red replied cheerfully, before turning his attention to Victor, "Please make sure all your cattle are branded. If you can get any of your neighbours to add cattle to your herd, make sure they are branded too."

"Dad wants to know why you want them?" Victor enquired.

"Tell him I can't say for what purpose. I'm trying to put together a herd of cattle of over five hundred, for a brief time."

"Can I come with our cattle?"

"Yes, and all those who allow their cattle to be included in the herd. You will be camping out, so bring food drays for possibly a week, but it must be kept totally secret."

"Red, you'll have to think up a reason for a gathering of cattle, for example to select some for showing somewhere?" Victor persisted.

"Right Victor, I'll run with the showing idea, use it in public if you are ever required to speak on this matter," Red smiled and said.

After clearing up this problem, general conversation resumed. Victor stayed the night and left early in the morning, to carry home the news of a police murder but not who Barry was in his private life, that was still secret. Steve and Bill left at the same time, crossing the creek and following a valley into the ranges. Jamie stayed behind, to keep Red company as he told Bill within the hearing range of Red, who instantly objected.

"Jamie, I'm old enough to look after myself, I'll have you know!"

They rode into the ranges, which brought back memories for Bill, who told Steve about his and Ian's patrol down the river over a year ago. He talked about the cave of bats and the ruined hut at the top of the hill. As Bill remembered and gave voice to these memories, he saw Steve smiling and wondered what he was thinking. A couple of times they were stopped by men who knew Steve as they rode deeper into the high hills.

"We're under observation." He commented as it dawned on him that he was riding into a high security area.

"We have been since we entered this region," Steve replied.

Turning a corner Bill recognised the lay of the land and as they rode further down the river, he saw the hill he and Ian had climbed with Bob Pringle. He was amazed to be riding up that same hill with Steve. At the top he saw a restored slab hut with a shingle roof and gardens all around it. Steve saw his amazement and smiled.

"You're about to meet my Mother and Father. I'll take my Mother inside and tell her. You will tell my Father when he asks you why you have come, but not that Barry was his son. Mother will do that later today," he said.

Bill was surprised at the change wrought on this flat area of land, half way up a tall hill, it was just amazing.

"It was prepared by Bob Pringle who employed a group of men," Steve explained.

"Where are those men now?" Bill enquired.

"Bob employed the men who wanted work to pay for their trip to the Victorian Gold Fields, ideal all round, wouldn't you say?"

"Clever of Bob to have achieved such a renewal from how I remember it."

They talked as they unsaddled their horses as a slim man in middle age approached them and greeted Steve, before turning towards Bill, as Steve introduced him.

"Father, this is Bill Todd, who has come to deliver some information to you. Bill, my father Inspector John Sefton."

Bill addressed him by his formal title, while Steve slipped away to find his Mother.

"So why have you come here Mr. Todd?"

"To tell you Sir, that Barry Hodge has been murdered."

"Has he now, how was he killed?"

"Sliced across his throat, a quick death, we believe he knew his killer."

Bill explained and answered questions clearly, and by the time the Inspector had completed his detailed questions, Bill was exhausted.

His condition must have been obvious, because the Inspector said, "Come lad, we'll go and have a cup of tea, if I can find my wife and Steve. You'd think the place was small and easy to find someone, but it isn't, not when they want to keep out of my way!"

"How do you do Mrs. Sefton," Bill said after Steve introduced his Mother.

"May I call you Bill?" she asked, after the usual greeting.

"Yes I'd like that."

"Now don't go away, stay while I tell John something I've kept secret from him because it wasn't the right time, but now it is."

"What is it Susie?" John asked.

"Barry was your eldest son, he did love you. He knew you would never have sent him to Hill Top if you had known he was your son."

John Sefton had paled and Steve handed him a mug of strong alcohol. Bill was shocked, as was all of them to see tears in his eyes. This man was noted for his strength and men like him didn't show emotion. Bill remembered that this was a very private gathering of family.

"We've kept so many secrets from each other and I'm going to be much happier when they are all revealed. I love my wife and my sons, I have always loved them, even when I didn't know of our relationship," John looked up at Bill and explained. He took a sip from the mug and continued, "I knew Barry was my son. He told me so the last time we met and I was able to give him a hug. He told me I was a grandfather and he asked me to keep an eye on his wife even if she was to marry again."

"You knew all the time about Barry's life?" Susie exclaimed in a surprised voice.

"Yes dearest, all of his story and I will be demanding to see my grandchildren too. Susie you have taken such good care of me, sometimes I think I don't deserve your love, but only sometimes."

Susie told him clearly what she thought of his words and they all laughed. They'd just completed a meal when the sound of a horse's hooves was clearly heard. Steve left the hut going outside to investigate and found Jamie unsaddling his horse. After completing this job, he entered the hut and handed the Inspector a paper. While he read it, Susie greeted Jamie with a hug and proceeded to fill a plate for him. John passed the note to Steve, who scanned the lines, and then gave it to Bill, who lost colour as he read it. Bill began to speak about this man's position in the Hill Top barracks.

"We've known him since the Closed Valley affair and he has been made head of our security in the barracks. I will need to leave here early in the morning to return to 'Red's Land', Ian and I must get back to our Sergeant and inform him of this new information," he said.

"What are you going to do about him?" John asked.

"Nothing, we'll watch and keep our 'powder dry' to see how he's operating," Bill replied, giving a grim smile.

"A man after my own heart!" The Inspector laughed and said, slapping Bill on his shoulder.

Bill left at first light with Jamie, who was known by the security men even in the gloom of the lower hills.

Chapter 28

Ian arrived back from his visit to the school house and impatiently waited another day for Bill to be escorted back from the ranges to 'Red's Land'. Both men had been to secret places and had asked permission to be able to talk to one another. Though each had been warned about how much of what they'd learnt could be passed on to Sergeant Green. The general consensus had been only the bare essential, which in Ian's report was the suspicion from the late Barry Hodge. Bill had been told about the life of Barry. "You may tell Mr. Percy," the Inspector said.

The central secret was the place where Bill had visited with Jamie for obvious reasons. The Inspector had said to Bill, "Our security has turned back many men seeking to explore these ranges, one day one of Frank's men will get through our security, but not yet, we aren't ready to fight that battle."

The older man had smiled at Bill in a way, which caused Bill to be relieved he was on his side in the coming conflict.

Red Bryant was happy to have his wife home again, she gave him all the news, plus the suspicion. He went silent for a few minutes, then looking up stated, "Charley Rush must be warned, along with Alex Pitt, if it isn't too late already?"

What kind of danger is Alex facing now?" Ian asked.

"Ian, Alex is in grave danger, the drug was meant to kill him, surely you were informed of the implications of that attack?" Red answered.

"I thought the whole point of the attack was that he'd seen Frank Black in the shanty, now it's well known, so what's the problem?"

Red brushed his red hair back with his hand and explained, "Alex hasn't been able to remember who Frank was talking to in the shanty."

"Has anyone asked Alex to give a description of what he saw in the shanty?" Bill enquired.

"Charley asked Alf to question Alex," Ian replied slowly.

"What did Alf say?"

"That Alex couldn't remember seeing anyone in the shanty, even Frank Black."

"So we only have Barry's word for Frank Black's presence in the shanty," Ian said thoughtfully.

There was sudden silence as Red sat up and stared at Ian, before saying, "Are you questioning the word of a dead colleague, by any chance Ian?"

"Ian, are you doubting Barry's observation?" Even Bill was surprised at his friend and asked.

"No Bill, but others will doubt him, after all he acted the fool in our barracks and we are unable to tell the truth about him. Red, what's keeping Alex alive?"

"The fact that he can't remember the two men he saw talking in the shanty. Alf has a reputation as an interrogator and any doubt in his mind about Alex knowing and keeping quiet would have caused his death, one way or another on the same day."

"Red, we need to get up to Hill Top, as soon as possible," Bill said.

"No, I don't think so, not you two today," Redreplied thoughtfully before calling out loudly, "Jamie!"

He arrived trying to catch his breath, "Yes Mr. Bryant."

"How would you like to ride up to Hill Top and pass on the suspicion to the good Sergeant and have a quiet word with Charley Rush, in the company of Ken?"

"Mr. Bryant" Ken asked after arriving and hearing his name spoken.

"Ken, Jamie, how many times do I have to tell you my name is Red," Red interrupted grimly.

Jamie took a big breath, moved a bit further away from the big man, and replied, "It's just that you're older and we were taught to be polite to your age group."

Bill turned a laugh into a cough, as Ian murmured, "Just as well he used the words 'age group' or there'd be blood on the floor!!"

"You call my wife Mary, so what's the difference?"

"She's young and not much older than we are," Jamie said, taking a step backward.

Mary beamed with pleasure, as Red enquired even more gently, "What is the difference?"

Jamie moved even further back and desperately looked around for help and finding none he said carefully, "You're the Boss."

"You weren't thinking that at all, you just thought it was a good way out of an awkward conversation," Red roared.

"We don't have any grey hairs in our beards," Jamie said in a moment of even greater courage or total loss of wit.

"Grey hairs are a sign of intelligence," Red said, enjoying himself and not to be out done.

"If you say so," Jamie replied, edging towards the doorway under the eyes of everyone in the room and with that he escaped.

"Now wasn't that fun, I'm married to a young woman," Red grinned at the assembly of faces.

"And I'm married to an old man!" Mary said and laughed.

The men left the room as Mary and Red talked to one another.

"We don't have any children, but lots of young sons," Bill heard Mary say.

"That's why I play with them, they are all brave young men. Like John Sefton, I know where the young men are going and I worry about their safety," Red added.

Bill repeated some of what he had heard to Ian as they walked across to the stables. They found Ken and Jamie saddling their horses.

"Mary said there's cooked meat in the smaller package in the kitchen," Kevin said, coming into the stables behind Bill and Ian.

"Thank her from us both please," Ken asked Kevin.

"I will Ken."

Kevin didn't leave the stables but helped the men prepare for the night ride.

"A long ride tonight?" he asked Ken encouragingly.

"Yes, and it's important to reach Hill Top as soon as we can."

"I know it's a long way Ken, but once you get tired stop even for a couple of hours of sleep. I know you have to get to your destination but if you're too tired you mightn't see danger."

Ken smiled and to the surprise of the other men, gave Kevin a hug, it was obvious to those watching it was normal to those two me.

"Keep safe lad," Kevin said.

"I will Kevin, Steve is the one who needs lectures!"

"He gets them too!"

"I think Kevin looks on Ken as the son he never had or couldn't have." Bill said quietly as Ken and Jamie rode out into the moonlight. "Kevin saved Ken's life in the 'Closed Valley', and Ken and Steve saved his life when the police invaded the valley."

"How far will they ride in the dark?" Ian asked Kevin.

"Difficult to say, Ken is the strong one. No fire or tea before dawn, a mug of tea and away again chewing cooked meat."

"Do you miss not sharing a cabin with Ken and Steve?"

"Hell no, they could never keep still, always up and doing something, and as I remember, generally thought I should be up too! But I do enjoy seeing those boys," he added.

They bid each other good night….Bill and Ian left at first light for Hill Top and rode steadily north all day, stopping when they needed to, making it a relaxed journey. In the late afternoon Bill chose a waterhole which looked as if it had the possibility of having fish in it. After settling the horses, Bill took a line and Ian made the fire, later Ian talked about his impressions of Harriet Hodge and her world.

"What will she do now?" he enquired.

"Marry a farmer I think. He will have to ask John Sefton for her hand in marriage, because of his two grandchildren."

"That could be rather daunting."

"Not if he's the right kind of man Bill."

Over the camp fire and eating a freshly cooked fish, Bill passed on some news.

"Bob Pringle and Betsy Hunt were married in late spring. Dick said the kitchen is more peaceful at the present time, but he's not putting money on how long it'll last!!"

"I want a few words with Bob the next time I see him," Ian mused.

"I doubt any of us will get any satisfaction, I'd forget about it," Bill laughed and uttered.

"Who was Barry Hodge?" Ian asked.

"Lionel Sefton, Susie farmed him out to a couple called David and Charlotte Hodge, who were unable to have children. David gave Barry his late father's name."

"When did he return to Susie?"

"They died of suspected typhus when he was fifteen years old. Their deaths hit him badly as it was a deeply loving family. He was aware Susie was his real Mother, as she had visited their cottage frequently, there was no jealousy in this relationship. Barry married Harriet at seventeen years."

"Murdered at twenty-six years," Ian added sadly.

Ian asked some more questions about where John and Susie were living which Bill found difficult to answer.

"Ian, I can't answer those questions, other than to say without the company of either Steve or Jamie I wouldn't have got within miles of their camp, the security is iron clad," he said regretfully.

Ian didn't pester Bill anymore, as he could see his friend had been instructed to remain silent about what he had seen in the ranges.

"When the time comes you and I will be riding into the ranges with Ken, Jamie or Steve but my lips are sealed until that time," Bill did say quietly.

"Did you request my company?"

"Of course I did. This subject is now closed. I'm for my swag."

Chapter 29

Jamie's one thought was to hand over the paper to Sergeant Green as soon as he reached Hill Top. He thought he'd made excellent time, hardly stopping at all after Ken had told him to ride as if the devil was behind him. He'd kept looking behind him to see if Ken was coming too and not being able to see him only added to his distress. They'd been stopped by men whom Ken had recognised as coming from the Black Creek camp.

"You ride and I'll hold them, get that paper to the Sergeant no matter what stands in your way," Ken had said.

He had ridden like the wind, pushing his horse and himself to get the paper into safe hands. Now he handed his horse to the Hill Top farrier who took one look at the man and said, "Don't worry Mr. Tyson, I'll unsaddle your horse and get your belongings to the visitors end of the barracks, your horse needs paddock time," as Jamie thanked him.

The farrier thought Mr. Tyson could do with sleep time too. He watched the exhausted man walk carefully up to the office. Sergeant Green looked up from the papers on his desk to see Jamie enter his domain. He had rarely seen such an exhausted man stagger in.

"Sit down Mr. Tyson before you fall down," he said.

He knew Jamie was on special duties so to enter his office in his present state meant trouble of some kind or another. In the few moments after Jamie had sat down and composed himself, the Sergeant noticed Jamie's hand shaking with effort as he extracted a paper from his pocket.

"Wait a moment," the Sergeant said.

He went to his doorway and called out to John Hale, who was near the stables, to fetch a mug of tea. John returned to the office with a mug of steaming tea from the kitchen and handed it to Jamie, who suddenly found he couldn't hold it, such was his exhaustion.

"Mr. Tyson…" the Sergeant began to say, reading the paper.

"Sergeant, is Ken Taylor here?" Jamie interrupted him.

"I haven't seen him, why would he be here Mr. Tyson?"

"We left 'Red's Land' together in the moonlight and stopped for a few hours' sleep around dawn but we rode into trouble in the late morning. Ken recognised a couple of men who had been in the Black Creek camp and he told me to ride like hell. I couldn't see him riding up behind me so I don't know where he is now if he isn't here?'

The Sergeant felt a cold shiver down his back as he thought of the Black Creek men roaming around his countryside, and the implications of the paper, which had been delivered to his desk.

"Take Mr. Tyson to the visitors bunk area of the barracks and see to his needs, then return here please Mr. Hale," The Sergeant instructed.

He watched John holding on to Jamie to stop him falling, as Jamie staggered out of his office. John managed to get him to the bunk, removing his boots and putting a blanket over him, but Jamie was almost instantly asleep. Returning to the office, he sat down in front of the Sergeant's desk and he was handed a paper.

"This is what Mr. Tyson brought for me, from Harriet Hodge's papers, this one being the last letter from her late husband."

"Barry was married?" John said without thinking, clearly in shock.

"With two children."

"I shouldn't have asked, my apologies Sergeant," John immediately said.

"No matter, alive no one was interested in him, now he's dead, secrets will slowly be revealed." He was silent for a few moments and then asked, "Mr. Hale, will you find Mr. Rush for me please?"

"Yes I'll try and find him but he isn't in the barracks."

"Try the doctor's tent," adding "Mr. Hale the contents of the paper must remain a secret even from your colleagues.'

"That is understood, Sergeant."

"Good man. Then return to me, there's another matter which will require you to go out on patrol, perhaps for a day or two."

John left the office deeply disturbed. He was now in a circle of knowledge, which was obviously part of a wider picture, but in these barracks only the Sergeant was aware of the whole nasty business. He wondered what else he was to learn this day once he found Charley, leaving the police area and entering the community of tents.

"May I see Mr. Rush please?" he asked an assistant at the medical tent.

"You'll find him out the back of the tent burning old dressings."

John walked around to the back of the dirty looking tent and saw Charley feeding a fire with pieces of wood. Charley looked up to see John, who was usually the most cheerful of all his colleagues with a serious expression on his face.

"What's up John? Have you been eating a F– sour lemon?" Charley asked.

"No Charley, I came to find you and Alex."

"Well you've found me, I'm doing this F– dirty job for one of them in the tent."

"Where's Alex, Charley?"

"How the hell should I know? Alf came and took him away for safety yesterday."

John felt cold, really cold. He asked, "When are you coming back to our barracks?"

"When I've completed burning this stinky stuff."

"When you do go back, call in at the office the Sergeant wants to see you."

"What's going on John?"

"I don't know."

He walked back to his barracks, the feeling of cold persisting as he entered the office and told the Sergeant what had transpired behind the tent.

"I don't think Charley ought to be told anything about that piece of paper, until we have proof," John said.

"I agree with you Mr. Hale. Mr. Rush is an unknown quantity in this equation, and I expect a dangerous one if he felt his friend's life was in danger, which we believe it is at this moment." The Sergeant stopped talking for a moment and spoke quietly, "The other matter, Mr. Taylor is missing."

He recounted all of what Jamie had told him, with particular emphasis on the movement of the men from the Black Creek camp.

"When did they leave their camp?" John asked.

"This is the first mention of these men and I don't like it. I'll send someone to check if any are still in the camp."

"Who are they Sergeant?" John asked.

"They're a group of about fifty men, whom we believe are under the instructions of Inspector Frank Black."

"This is the connection to Hill Top. Sergeant are you intending to warn us of a possible threat to the community?"

"I take your point, not yet, we have to be careful of the implications of that paper. I'd rather he remain in ignorance of our knowledge, the life of Alex may depend upon it"

"Very well Sergeant, you have my silence."

"You will of course continue to investigate anything connected to this matter and keep me informed please. Now to this more pressing matter of the missing Mr. Taylor. I want you to ride back down the track, if you get far enough, you will meet Mr. Todd and Mr. Percy, who are returning from 'Red's Land'. They are to assist you in locating him, for this reason take more than you will need in rations."

John left the office and went to see how Jamie was doing and was pleased to find him still asleep, knowing full well if he'd been awake, he would've wanted to come with him, not knowing what state Ken could be in after being in the hands of these men.

Within an hour after leaving the Sergeant's office, John was riding down the southern track.

Chapter 30

John rode well into the afternoon before he saw Bill and Ian riding towards him, and felt a sinking feeling that Ken wasn't with them. Surely they would've seen some sign of Ken on their way north. They met up under some trees near the track and John explained his problem. It was at this point that he learnt that it had been Bill and Ian who had made the original report about the fake gold mining at Black Creek.

"Did Jamie say where they'd been held up?" Ian asked.

"Yes, though he was a bit vague about it, he said the place was near a creek crossing that Steve had told him where he'd got drenched in flooded waters."

"You know Ian, the crossing in flood waters, when we first took Steve down to Red to be taught to be a stockman," Bill explained.

"That creek is on the edge of the ranges; why were they riding up that way?"

"Jamie said to avoid the travellers, he thought it would be safer to ride that way than the usual track that was used by everyone."

"He must have known this way wasn't in the least safe," Bill said with a surprised expression on his face.

"It would've been safe in ordinary circumstances, perhaps no one knew the men from the Black Creek were in the area," Ian said quietly, adding, "Do you know of any way that we can make contact with the security men in the ranges?"

"No, except by riding into the ranges, as I remember we hadn't ridden too far before we were confronted by horsemen."

"We'll try it, but well before the place Ken disappeared on the edge of the ranges."

"Are you happy to come along with us?" Ian asked, turning in his saddle to face John.

"Yes, of course I'll come with you."

John informed his two colleagues about Alex being taken by Alf, to a place of safety, but he wouldn't say where the place was situated. This was disturbing news, and each man rode in silence concerned about the welfare of Alex. They stopped riding in early twilight and made camp as usual beside a waterhole. John was accustomed to seeing Ian dive into the water, after he'd checked that it was safe to do so. John was happy to follow suit and wash the dust out of his hair and beard, he liked the feeling of being clean. Later the warmth of the fire and companionship finished the day. They left the camp before sunrise, turning east and reached the ranges in the late afternoon and camped at the edge of a long valley. They left early in the morning and rode down the valley towards the hills. Gradually the hills became steeper as they rode through rough country.

"I feel we're being observed," Bill said, giving voice to their thoughts.

"For some time I think, I have that itchy feeling on the back of my neck of something I can't see, watching me," John added.

They came to a fork in the track within the hills with a choice of directions.

"Let's go south, this way will give us the best chance of being found by the right people," Bill said.

They rode beside the river for about two miles, which was not always easy with logs and big rocks, sometimes having to ride up a hill and down again to avoid the steep edges of the water. All the while they rode south, until on turning a corner they came face to face with three men blocking their track, two of whom Bill recognised.

"What are you doing here Mr. Todd?" one of the men asked.

Bill introduced Ian and John, then explained their problem which was news to the men. John also imparted the news about Alex which was received with shock.

"Come with us to our camp, your news is important, and with Ken missing we need a direction on how we'll deal with the situation," one of them said after they'd had a quiet talk with each other.

One of the men rode south at speed and was out of sight in minutes. Bill, Ian and John rode behind the two men, in and out from behind high hills, always at ground level. This was a security detail and they were being taken to a camp, round and round hills, going one way and then another, even turning back and going the other way.

"We used to do what you are trying to achieve in India when I was a boy in that army. Sometimes it works, but only if the troops are unobservant. We are trained observers, I could draw you a map of where we have been today," Ian said to one of the men.

"We wondered if you knew what we were doing Mr. Percy?" he said, turning in his saddle.

"Just thought I'd mention it."

"Do you have your small brass telescope in your saddle bag?"

"Yes I do."

"We would like to borrow it if you don't mind."

"I have no objection if you're careful in using it. Ken is a friend as well as a colleague."

"To us Mr. Percy, he is an important part of our team. We think he saw the danger to our operation and tried to reach us and warn us that the men of the Black Creek were in our area. What's their purpose to be here is the question."

"How long have you known of our entry into the ranges?" John asked, changing the subject.

"From the moment you entered the high hills, Mr. Hale."

"You know our names?" John said in surprise.

"Of course we know all the Hill Top police," he heard a laugh and the voice replied.

"I know that voice too!" John rode in silence for a moment or two, before saying, "I thought you might John, but no names today."

"You were very good at your job at Green Hills."

"They've chosen the best men available for this operation."

Bill and Ian had listened to this conversation with interest as they rode into a police camp. None of them were in the least surprised to see Red Bryant, in the midst of a group of men, as he stood up and came forward.

"Why am I not surprised to see you three men ride into this camp?" he remarked.

"Perhaps because we care what happened to Ken as much as you do Red," Ian replied.

"A very strong observation Ian. Now if you will lend your small telescope to this man, we may be able to discover where Ken is being held?"

Ian showed the policeman his telescope and aspects of it and watched him leave with two of his colleagues.

"It seems odd talking around a fire, knowing names and not using them," Bill observed.

"We listen to men in other camps and collect their names. It's possible that men listen at our camps. It's better for us to remain unknown," John's friend replied.

"Ken?" Bill asked.

"If they even suspect that he's a member of our operation, they will want answers. We must find him before they get busy torturing him."

An hour later the men returned and handed the telescope back to Ian. They conferred away from the camp out of their visitors hearing, then a number of men left the camp. John's friend returned to the fire and sat down.

"They've located the camp where Ken is being held captive," he said then continued, "Our men move like shadows and I suspect we'll see Ken sometime tonight. We also hope to take one of their men captive and question him as to their intentions here."

"Do you mean to question him here?" John asked.

"No, we have another place for that. Before you leave here we'll pass on to you any useful information for Sergeant Green."

Having no choice, as it was late in the day, Bill, Ian and John camped the night with the men. At the first light of the new day, they were aware of the nameless men returning to the camp. The fire was stoked with wood as they surrounded it, waiting for water to boil and make tea. All the men were silent with grim expressions.

"Do I assume your colleagues don't talk at breakfast?" John enquired of his friend.

"Not until at least mid-day, just like Bill and Ian!" He laughed quietly and replied.

"You have my sympathy!"

The two men stopped talking as a horseman rode into the camp, dismounted and handed the reins of his horse to the nearest man. He walked to the fire and was handed a mug of tea, after his first sip, he looked at the three Hill Top policemen.

"Red has taken Ken home to 'Red's Land,' he's bruised from rough treatment. They were waiting for another man to arrive, to question Ken in a more serious manner. His captors will have now discovered the bare trunk of the tree as we took him during the night. Ken wasn't able to tell us much about the men from Black Creek other than that they were looking forward to a raid on something. What it is we don't know." He smiled and continued.

"What do we tell Jamie Tyson?" Bill enquired.

"Tell him to ride to 'Red's Land' and keep out of trouble!"

"It follows him round like a dog!!" Ian smiled cheerfully.

Laughter rolled across the camp, which was quite unique so early in the day. They were escorted out of the ranges by a northern route and camped within the hills, before riding out on to the open grasslands leading up to Hill Top. Jamie was almost undone with relief at hearing Ken was safe and left the next day for 'Red's Land', though he hadn't recovered properly from his northern ride.

"Nothing but chains could've kept him here!" The Sergeant said to John as he watched him leave.

Chapter 31

John, Bill and Ian had returned to the peaceful existence of Hill Top. Their report of the men from Black Creek didn't seem to have any meaning, just like gold miners going from camp to camp. Ian and Bill spent many hours writing reports, covering their recent activities. Life had changed in the barracks since George Nash had resigned some weeks ago. Ian was completing his report, as his Sergeant came to the door of his office.

"If you're finished using my desk, please come outside. I want to address the men," he said.

Ian had been expecting an interruption ever since he'd heard of the arrival of new police at the barracks.

Once they were all gathered together, or at least those who were not out on patrol, the Sergeant introduced Harry White and Nick Rose, both ex-stockman and Rex Howard, an ex-blacksmith. The three men were young, strong and fitted into their uniforms with ease, but it was Rex who instantly drew the eyes of his colleagues, because of his obvious strength honed at the forge. He out shone all the men present with his skin tight white pantaloons, blue shirt and shiny black knee boots. A tinge of jealousy was felt by his colleagues, who were all in various ways attractive men, but Rex put them in the shade as they instinctively knew all the girls would be drawn to him. They were to gradually discover that Rex had a sunny disposition and men naturally liked him. A couple of his colleagues took him to the various food tents, in the hope he'd put on weight but his shape didn't change and this idea was soon dropped. Rex knew what they were doing, as he had experienced the same type of behaviour from his mates in Sunny Flat!

On his first night meeting up with Willie, they went into the community and ate a meal at Ma Shell's food tent. She instantly loved him as Willie had expected, to his amusement and the jealous disgust of all the men present! They then went to the best grog shanty and down to the tent at the end of the row. This was the crowning event for Willie and he laughed so much that his sides hurt! The moment the girls caught sight of Rex all their other clients may as well have gone home, including Bill and Ian, who were not in the least amused. The brothel keeper saw money running out of the tent flap and was furious with his girls. They dealt quickly with their regular clients, including Bill and Ian, who put up a fight for proper attention but lost the battle, to their utter disgust. Willie and Rex had the best girls for the night and Willie was praised for bringing a clean and wonderful specimen of male strength to their establishment.

As might have been expected their employer was on the Sergeant's doorstep the next morning to complain about the police. The Sergeant could hardly wait for the irritating man to leave, so he could have a good laugh and thought 'oh to be young again', but those days had long gone. Now he'd have to reprimand his men for being normal. He sent out a call to Bill, Ian, Willie and Rex to come to his office.

"Gentlemen, life has been quiet in Hill Top for some weeks until last night, the brothel keeper has been here this morning complaining about your behaviour last night. Mr. Percy did you have to put a bag over his head and did you Mr. Todd push him into a tub of water, to cool him down?" he asked putting on a serious face.

"It did cool him down, he was getting very red in the face!" Bill replied.

"Mr. Darkwood and Mr. Howard, he asked me to ban you from his tent, but he didn't say why, so please enlighten me," The Sergeant continued while keeping a straight face.

Neither Bill nor Ian had been expecting this question and waited with considerable interest to hear Willie's reply.

"I think because the girls much preferred the young men to the old ones!!" Willie looked straight ahead and answered.

The Sergeant was enjoying himself after a quick glance at the faces of Ian and Bill and couldn't resist another question.

"Who do you think could be thought of as old?"

"You'd have to ask the girls, Sergeant." Willie replied carefully, seeing a chasm opening up at his feet.

"Very well, you may go now gentlemen, please refrain from causing trouble in the future."

In the barracks Bernie Sharp was in a foul mood, after being turned out of the tent last night by his regular girl. He swore he'd get even with that bastard Darkwood as soon as he saw him. As Willie walked into the eating room Bernie made a lewd comment about Rex, who before he could respond, saw Willie punch Bernie on the jaw, who fell heavily between two tables in the eating room. There was a grim silence as Bernie jumped up and withdrew his knife, which he kept razor-sharp, amid cries from astounded men.

"Use your fists, shame, use your fists."

Bernie had no intention of being hurt again and struck out at Willie, who received a nasty cut on his shoulder. Rex moved like lightning and struck Bernie in the face and in the next action disorientated him as his knife fell from his hand. A furious Bernie tried to pick up it up but was no match for Rex, who pushed him out of the way and sent him sprawling on the floor. Rex took the knife and hurled it with considerable strength sending it deeply into one of the roof beams.

"Get it if you can," he said, looking at Bernie.

Bernie backed away from Rex calling him every name he could lay his tongue to. Rex stood and laughed as Bernie left the room still calling him names. In the meantime Ian and Bill had taken Willie to the community medical tent.

As no one was available to attend to Willie, Sergeant Green was asked for his opinion.

"The closest doctor is my brother-in-law. Mr. Hale will you take Mr. Darkwood out to the Hade farm?" he said.

"Yes Sergeant."

"You'd better take the dray as well as your own horse. Mr. Darkwood is well bandaged and ought to make a good trip."

"Sergeant, it's a long way and the dray will be rough. I'd like to suggest one of the horses, plus Nick Rose. The cut isn't deep, but it needs stitching as soon as possible."

Horses were chosen and John, Willie and Nick left the barracks.

One other policeman who had watched the fight, thought it was an ideal time to create more mayhem in the barracks. He smiled as he'd seen the knife quiver in the ceiling beam, it was such a good blade, better than his own knife. He found Bernie at the rear of the barracks and as no one was in sight he would've liked to have played with him, but there wasn't enough time.

"Did you see what that bastard did to me?" Bernie asked.

"You're a fool Bernie."

The older man grasped Bernie who began to struggle in fear, he tried to speak in the sudden realization of what was coming to him when he saw the knife. For Bernie his life ended, just the way he'd taken Barry's life.

The shock which ran through the barracks when the body of Bernie Sharp was discovered with his throat cut, was a lot better than the policeman had expected of his colleagues. It was most satisfying to see them in shock and a type of disorientation gripped the barracks. This way they wouldn't be on guard as usual. All the men were accounted for in the investigation that followed the murder. His plan was working well. Men were still being sent out on patrols, as he watched Bill, Ian and that stupid boy Rex go out to Ma Shell's food tent. They were due to leave in the early afternoon and go somewhere, he did hope it was days away from Hill Top.

As always the men carried a swag and rations, Bill and Ian decided to take Rex with them to get him away from the barracks. Their job involved visiting a squatter a few miles from the settlement. A number of his sheep had recently been stolen, which was to be a simple matter and they expected to be back before dark. It didn't turn out that way because the squatter's wife was about to give birth with their first baby and he didn't know what to do. Rex was able to assist in this matter as he'd helped in a delivery at Sunny Flat. The squatter and his wife were deeply grateful to the police for their help in knowing exactly what was needed to bring their son into the world.

As it was too late to return to the settlement they camped near a waterhole in the early twilight,

"Even though it's only about two hours riding to Hill Top, it's better to ride in the daylight, except of course for the early mornings," Bill explained to Rex.

The next morning after they'd finished the first meal of the day, Bill and Ian were surprised to see the man who worked for Ma Shell arrive in a dray at their camp.

"I'm glad I caught you. Ma Shell sent me to tell you not to return to Hill Top in your police uniforms or on your horses, we've been invaded," he told the surprised Policemen.

He went on to say that Ma had told him that the invaders were the men from the Black Creek gold mine and they'd taken over the barracks and the community at Hill Top.

"How did you know where we were?" Bill asked.

"Willie told me to tell Ma if she asked me, and to tell her something was badly wrong. Willie thought valuables ought to be hidden while there was still time," the man answered Bill and pointed at Rex.

"Why didn't you say something yesterday before we left Hill Top?" Ian said to Rex.

"Willie said not to say a word, because it isn't proof. You see Mr. Percy, where Bernie was killed could be seen from the medical tent. Willie thinks he saw the killing and who did it but he can't be absolutely sure that he isn't making a mistake."

"Rex, why Ma?" Bill enquired.

"Willie often told me, that for all her love of handsome men, she is a clever woman who knows a good deal about the local community. She'd be able to warn other people to hide their valuables."

"What is your part of Ma's message?" Ian enquired of the Ma Shell's workman.

"Ma instructed me to bring you old clothes and boots, I was then to take your police clothes, saddles, horse equipment and horses, to the squatter called Stuart Cameron. Do you know him?"

"Yes we do, he makes the worst whisky I've ever tasted!" Ian laughed,

"Ma said he'll look after your property. She also instructed me to tell you when you walk into the community, go to the girls' tent and keep out of sight, or you'll get locked up."

"Ma sent a rider to Green Hills last night. He'd been passing through on his way north and stopped for a bowl at Ma's tent."

"How did he get away?"

"It was as the men were securing the barracks and locking up the Police. Now if you don't mind, please change clothes and let me get on my way home," The man requested, clearly uneasy.

"What do you want to do?" Bill looked at Ian and asked.

"We'll follow Ma's plan until we get to Hill Top and see what's happening in the community."

The clothes Ma had chosen for Rex and his colleagues, which caused Ian to say, "Rex, these are clothes worn by men who work in the cesspits, the girls will run from you now!!"

Bill and Ian laughed. Rex refrained from stating the obvious when he looked at them in the same attire, thinking that Ma was clever to make people stay away from them.

"Ma sent this cooked meat, you might like to eat as you walk to the settlement?" The man suggested, gathering up their property.

Rex hid a smile, as Ian reluctantly agreed to this idea but he didn't hide it quick enough and Bill saw it.

Rex was aware that for all of their attention to the plan, Bill and Ian didn't like having two junior policemen keeping knowledge to themselves, then making a plan of action with a non- police person.

It was no surprise when Bill said, "In the future Rex, never tell anyone where we are going out of the community, or even in it. Our work is always secret, also don't call Ian 'Mr. Percy', you're one of us now."

"Very well Mr. Todd."

"You've been spending too much time in the company of Willie Darkwood!!"

"He's my friend, and I can hardly wait to tell him that you and Ian are wearing the clothes of unwashed cesspit workers!!"

"I hope you can swim Rex, because I can see a good dipping on your horizon!" Ian commented after squashing something on his arm.

Chapter 32

Alex Pitt woke up from his drugged sleep, with the clear memory of a colleague forcing him to drink a mug of nasty medicine, except it was the same taste he'd had from his quart-pot. He'd been told it would help him get better. He'd remembered looking up into the man's eyes, and they'd told another story, but he'd been too weak to escape from those powerful arms.

He looked around the wooden slabbed room where he was lying and discovered his leg was chained to a ring set in the wall and was lying on a dirt floor which was usual in slab dwellings. There was no furniture of any kind except a digging instrument. He wondered what it was for in this small space. He smiled as he understood, it was to create his own cesspit and bury it again.

He was in his uniform, or bits of it, without his boots. He had a barrel of water and nothing else. Alex had been aware of a man telling him to eat and forcing food down his throat. How many days he'd been there he didn't know but he felt it hadn't been that long.

Alex began to think what had led him to be captured. For the first time in days he had a clear memory of what he'd seen in the shanty. He'd seen with shock a colleague talking to Frank Black, giving the impression of being friends and he knew he had to get back to Hill Top in a hurry. His companion, that idiot Barry Hodge, had dared to question him on what he'd seen in the room. He didn't tell him, because he might say the name without thinking, as he usually did in the barracks.

He remembered Charley telling him that Barry had been murdered. It didn't make sense, why murder a useless policeman? He heard someone coming, the door was thrust open and two men were pushed in, also wearing chains. Alex recognised Tom Hunt and one of his security men called Jack. They'd been drugged and an non-descript man in shabby clothes, attached their chains to the ring in the wall.

"Don't get too comfortable, you're all going to be moved shortly," he said seeing that Alex was awake.

He laughed as he closed the door, leaving a bowl of food for the men, which didn't look at all clean, a bit like a dogs dish Alex thought, and wondered if he would ever see his friend Charley again.

Chapter 33

Sergeant Green sent a message to a squatter called Stuart Cameron to ask for assistance. He wished to borrow three quality horses who could walk between four and five miles an hour as Police horses were cheaper animals who could only manage two to three miles per hour on a daily basis. He explained that Willie Darkwood had a knife wound and he needed to make this trip, with all possible speed. His fear was if his policeman was to develop an infection it could turn a simple wound into a serious one. Stuart Cameron was only too happy to supply three of his fine horses.

John, Nick and Willie left Hill Top in the late morning on a long trip to the Hade farm. In the first hours John was amazed at how far they had travelled, the horses were magnificent. Willie was holding up a lot better than John had expected, though there was something bothering him.

"Nick, where did you do most of your stockwork?"

"Between Hill Top and Green Hills."

"So you could find your way from here to Green Hills easily?"

"Yes, almost blindfolded, it's lovely country," Nick laughed and replied.

"What's on your mind Willie?" John enquired.

"Trouble in Hill Top, probably now."

Nick poured tea into the waiting mugs near the fire which were the tops of the quart-pots and were never far away from the fire. With the mugs in their hands, they settled down, leaning against a couple of logs and John asked Willie to continue.

"Before I returned to the barracks this morning, I'd been told quite a few men were seen approaching the settlement from different directions, as if they were closing off all tracks to the settlement. When we left this morning, there were men watching from among the trees beside the track."

"Were you able to pass on this information?" John asked.

"Yes to Rex, I told him to tell Ma Shell when he went for a meal at midday."

"But you didn't tell anyone else Willie?"

"No, because there was a stranger in the medical tent, whom I think was one of the men checking me out."

"Do you want me to ride to Green Hills and request some police to make a visit to Hill Top?" Nick asked Willie.

"Yes please Nick, they needn't make a song and dance about it, just come to check all is well in the community, and you can report the murder," John said. "Willie, tomorrow will be a long day in the saddle, from before sunrise to twilight, can you manage it?" John asked, looking at Willie.

"I think so John, we've got friends back in the barracks, for them I can do it."

"What do you think?" John looked at Nick and asked.

"On this horse I can make the ride shorter, I know the country and can take short-cuts from here."

"When do you want to leave?" John enquired.

"Don't worry about me, I'm accustomed to long hours in the saddle, I'll leave when I wake up."

"Nick avoid trouble if you can and remember we don't own the horses!" John said, handing him his rations.

"I can take care of myself and the horse. If Willie's correct. we've had a murder."

By the time John was awake before sunrise the next day Nick had already left the camp. John was feeling disturbed that he didn't hear him leave. He was a light sleeper and didn't think anyone could go without him hearing their departure.

The next day was a long one and by nightfall, Willie had no colour in his face. They had travelled a lot further than usual and John expected to reach the farm in early twilight.

Chapter 34

Bill and Ian began to walk to the settlement and were followed by Rex, who hummed a tune he'd heard somewhere, until Bill told him to be quiet. Willie had warned him that they could be difficult saying, "It's probably something to do with being old!"

Rex thought Bill and Ian could be in their late twenties, which from the perspective of the young constables was getting on in the years, in other words, old! Rex enjoyed the walk in the sunshine, though he didn't like the clothes he was wearing or the insects which were attracted to it. He smiled as he saw Bill and Ian constantly shrouded in clouds of insects.

"What are you so happy about?" Bill asked Rex looking behind and seeing him smiling.

"Walking in the sunshine Bill"

"Keep your eyes peeled for trouble."

"Yes Bill."

As they approached the settlement they came upon a couple of men who seemed to be guarding the track. They hadn't seen anyone coming from the same direction as these three travellers.

"What's ya' business?" One of the men asked, stepping out from under a tree on to the middle of the track.

"What's it smell like?" Bill responded.

"Lots of old bones in this place." The man said, taking one whiff and waving them through.

"Dead or alive?" Ian enquired.

"Get away and take that stink with you," the man said, backing towards his friends.

They walked into the community behind the tents to the bottom one, They all seemed to be doing good business, on the surface, but before they reached the bottom tent they realised the men and women from the Black Creek weren't paying for anything in the settlement. On reaching the bottom tent, they were met by the cook, who pushed them into a side tent.

"Wait here."

"I must say you do stink!" Ma Shell said with a laugh as she arrived a few minutes later, as Ian ground his teeth. "They're looking for valuables and taking whatever they want from the people," she added.

"How are the merchants coping?" Ian asked.

"Mr. Charlie Wickham and his nasty wife were pushed into that old low cesspit last night for complaining. A few other men joined them, much to the delight of those who had watched the dipping!"

"Our Sergeant will be getting lots of complaints when they leave here!" Bill said expressing his thoughts.

"They haven't bothered Mrs. Green, but I'm told they ransacked the Sergeant's office, looking for papers and a brass telescope."

"Did they find it?" Ian asked.

"No, but they made a big mess I'm told, nor did they locate the papers, they're still searching for them."

"And our colleagues?"

"All locked up and out of harm's way. Some of the Creek men wanted to kill them, but others with calmer heads said lock them up," Ma grinned cheerfully.

"What can we do?" Ian asked.

"Walk around the tents, no one will bother you if they get too close, that is!" She grinned adding, "Walk separately and don't draw attention to yourselves."

"Ma can we get a feed at your place?" Rex enquired.

"Come to the back of my tent, but not all together."

Bill walked up the line of tents and stopped outside the tea room, to see the owners, Mother and daughter, serving tea and cakes to rude men and women. The younger girl seemed to be afraid and with good reason, as Bill noticed one of the men groping her and another man, pulling her on to his lap saying, "Give us a kiss girl"

She gave them tears instead and they laughed at her discomfort. Bill could do nothing to help her as he walked on making his way slowly up past other tents, to see other abuses being enacted on a community, who were helpless. Some of the more unpleasant locals joined in on the fun and Bill noted their names for later. Ian had been recognised by some of the leading members of the community..

"Keep your women and girls out of sight, and young attractive boys too," he was able to warn them.

As some of the men were shocked that he'd mentioned their sons, Ian replied, "Don't be dumb, abuse is abuse, you know it goes on in the community. The Black Creek men take what they want for gratification regardless of which one takes their eye."

The men were embarrassed and a letter was sent to Sergeant Green on this matter.

Rex wandered towards the horses, which he saw had been locked up in the police yard. He loved horses and they always sensed his care of them. As he examined them, he saw they hadn't been looked after properly, they all needed a good feed of quality grass. He looked to see where the police horses were situated and saw them in the lower paddock which had water at the bottom of it. As no one was guarding the horses Rex slipped into the yard, opened the gate and walked into the paddock. As he had expected, the horses followed him, spreading out in obvious delight at the abundance of rich green grass.

He watched the horses for a time, before slipping away amongst the trees to the back of the barracks, keeping out of sight of the men guarding the police prisoners. He was quite a distance from the rear end of the barracks, when he heard two men talking. He carefully parted some bushes and what he saw caused Rex to back away as quietly as he could to find Bill or Ian.

"Come with me, there's something you need to see?" He said after he'd found Ian.

Ian didn't feel like being co-operative to a junior policeman and made his position clear.

"Rex, I'm busy checking out our community," he said.

"Ian this is a community matter, please come before it's too late."

"No Rex, you can tell me later."

"If I do it later you probably won't believe me."

"That's very likely true."

Ian knew he was being unreasonable and difficult to young Rex. As he walked he began to wonder what Rex had found which he wanted to share with him. On a whim Ian decided to follow Rex and without seeming to do so, saw him crawl into some bushes. Curious he followed and was shocked to see the two men talking and he recognised Frank Black. The other man had his back to Ian, but the voice he recognised. He heard enough to know this was a planned attack

"It's progressing as well as could be expected, the men are behaving as commanded," the other man said.

The men moved away and Ian wasn't able to hear any more of their conversation. On the other hand Rex was close enough to hear the end of the conversation. He was unaware of Ian's presence. He thought he'd tell Ma because Willie trusted her. The two men parted and the policeman walked back to the barracks, thinking his job was finally completed and he could join Mr. Black.

Meanwhile Bill saw a little man coming towards him, whom the community called Weasel, the man laughed and called out loudly, "What'a ya know, a Hill Top policeman, not locked up."

Instantly Bill was grabbed by the men who had heard Weasel's cry of identity of a lone policeman and was roughly handled for a few minutes, before being frog marched to the lock-up.

Weasel was told by a member of the community, "If you don't disappear, we'll put you in the cesspit which is about to be filled in."

"If you're still alive!" Weasel laughed and replied before calling out to one of the Black Creek men saying, "This man has just threatened me for telling you about the mounted policeman."

"Did he now, that was stupid of him."

He raised his gun and shot him dead and walked down between the tents, to the sound of Weasel's laughter. Unfortunately the whole scene had been witnessed and Weasel's days were numbered. By the end of the day, Weasel had vanished, he would be located in a different state in time. Ian was caught later in the day, also betrayed by a man who hated him. As usual a message was passed on quietly to Ma Shell, who noted the man's name.

When Rex arrived at the back of the food tent for a bowl of thick soup, Ma was able to tell him

"You are the only one free, Mr. Todd and Mr. Percy were betrayed by two different local men."

"What will happen to those men?"

"Rex, that's community business."

"It's probably better that I don't know Ma."

"Yes Mr. Howard it's better that way," she grinned and said.

"What's going on tonight, there's a lot of activity?" Rex asked.

"They've acquired a number of drays and are loading them up with stuff they've stolen, we think they are leaving tonight. You'd better lie low for a few hours Rex, until they've really gone, then find a place to sleep."

He left with a full stomach and a slice of damper with honey. Being young, Rex had no intention of missing all the interesting activities surrounding him and he enjoyed watching the Black Creek men. There were fights over stolen articles and some of their women were just as bad as their men, stealing from the women of Hill Top. He couldn't understand why they were leaving at night and asked one of the men

"Cause we was told by the Boss, we gotta go east now where the F— hell is my woman?"

"I don't know," Rex answered.

He moved into the shadows thinking of his last conversation with Ma.

"Do you think Willie will be at the Hade farm now?"

"Yes, with those fast horses, which were borrowed from Mr. Cameron. He is probably having a meal with them. Don't you worry about Willie, that boy has more brains than is good for him!" she said, laughing at something but wouldn't tell him what it was.

As Rex stood in the shadow of a tent, watching out for trouble, he wondered what was happening in Willie's life?

Chapter 35

John Hale and Willie Darkwood arrived at the Hade Farm on the late afternoon of the second day after leaving Hill Top which was a record time as it usually took three full days. They'd had one camp and in the early morning Willie had to find a log to be able to mount his horse. They were met at the farm stables by Andrew and Shaun, who were immensely impressed with the two mares, as they were obviously not police horses to have made such a trip. Toby and Patrick were equally inspired with the fast-walking horses and talked about the various features evident in these animals. John and Willie found themselves secondary to their transport to the farm and felt rather proud to have been riding such lovely horses. John was rather pleased at the interest the Hade boys showed in the horses, because they'd be looked after properly, as one day they'd have to be returned to their owner. Toby and Shaun were directed to brushing them down before taking them to the horse paddock by their father, once he'd arrived at the stables.

The boys had been aware that Willie was to be seen by their father, but their love of horses had won their total interest until he drew their attention to helping Willie dismount. Andrew and John walked either side of Willie from the stables, down the side of the homestead to what was called the meat room.

"I feel much better," Willie declared at first glance.

Around the walls were all manner of instruments, a combination of tools for cutting up beasts or attending to wounds on humans. In the middle of the room was a large heavy log sliced in half, with leather straps hanging from it in various places. Willie didn't like the look of this bench, it appeared somehow threatening, like going somewhere not of one's choice. Sam was quite accustomed to seeing this expression on the faces of his patients, including his own children, when they had hurt themselves badly.

"We've all been on this table, it's usually the result of having a good time that ended in Dad having to fix us, so I can tell you he's had a lot of practice at keeping us alive and well!"

Willie wasn't keen on it even with Andrew's encouraging words, nevertheless he was helped up on to the bench.

"Bite on this stick while I examine you," Mr. Hade said to him with a gentle smile.

Andrew and John held him still, while the dressings were removed and blood seeped out from various places along the wound.

"I'll clean it, sew it up and you'll be as good as new when it heals up again," he explained to Willie.

Willie didn't share his cheerful opinion and was inclined to be uncooperative.

"What do you think, a large glass of alcohol?" Mr. Hade asked John.

"Definitely, what have you in mind?"

"Rum always did the trick in the army."

"I don't like rum" Willie said.

"Willie, I really ought to address you as Mr. Darkwood, but John tells me you'd rather be called by your Christian name. This is going to hurt and rum will deaden most of the pain, so what's it to be?" Mr. Hade said.

"Rum!" Willie said, sighing quietly.

Biting the stick helped, the rum made him feel sick, and he was sure he'd felt every stitch pulled threw his skin. He had Andrew on one side and John on the other, talking to him like he was three years old! It seemed to go on for a very long time, before Mr. Hade spoke to him.

"All over Willie, that only took an hour. John and Andrew will stay with you until the dinner bell rings. We'll eat early and you may as well come to our table, you'll feel groggy, but don't be concerned, we are quite accustomed to having people in that state, including our sons at various times."

At the table Andrew and John sat either side of him. It was a happy gathering of the cheerful Hade family, as John remembered from his time here after the Black Mountain problem.

"I saw our neighbours today and they told me they'd heard voices coming out of that old gold mining place on the other side of Black Mountain," Andrew said during the meal.

"Ghosts you mean?" Patrick asked.

"They thought the voices were coming out of the Bone shaft. They went and looked down it and it was all silent, they told me it felt eerie," Andrew replied.

Sam Hade happened to be watching Willie, whose face suddenly changed to white. Willie no longer saw Toby across the table, but the face of the Old Man.

"Old Man," he murmured softly.

Everyone at the table stopped talking and sent questioning expressions to the head of the table.

"Why are you seeing him?" Sam asked.

"He wants me to remember something, he says it's important, it's in the shadows of my mind, but I can't quite see it."

The rum was also having an effect and Sam's gentle prompting brought more of his memory to the surface of his mind.

"I heard through the crack in the slab wall in the barracks. Bernie was talking to someone, near my bunk," Willie said.

"What did you hear, Willie?"

"I heard Bernie say, 'They'll be happy in the Bone shaft, all bones together.' The Old Man told me to remember it."

The whole table of people were quite suddenly shocked into a silence and waited with bated breath as Sam asked, "Willie, who's in the Bone Shaft?"

Willie was close to going to sleep as he mumbled, "Alex Pitt, and, and, I can't..."

Both Andrew and John took hold of him as a deep sleep overcame Willie. He was taken to a bed which had been made ready for him in the visitor's area. There was another bunk in the same room for John. After he'd been put to bed, they all returned to the main room in the house, to decide on their course of action.

"Did I hear correctly that Alex Pitt is missing?" Sam asked John.

"Yes Mr. Hade."

"Now we know where he's to be found."

"How deep is the Bone Shaft?" John enquired.

"Fourteen feet deep and about six feet wide at the bottom, according to Toby."

"How does Toby know?" Andrew began to ask.

"Not now, Andrew, I'll explain later," his Father said.

"The gold miners, unknowingly, began to search for gold in an ancient Burial Ground, hence the Bone shaft," He explained, turning to John.

"I'll get the rope ladder," Toby said.

"What rope ladder?" Andrew asked.

Again his father said, "Don't ask Andrew, I'll explain on our way to the old gold field."

The whole household spent the next couple of hours preparing for an early morning ride with the dray and equipment.

A long way away, an Old Man sat in front of his fire and smiled; the boy remembered. As Willie had seen him, he had, in turn, seen Willie, it was as if they had been facing one another in a split second of time. The boy had looked into his eyes and remembered, just like any of his own people. The Old Man smiled as he thought of the happy boys who had cheerfully come to his aid in the burial ground. Now they'd fill in the shaft and his ancestors would be at peace again. He smiled as he gazed into his fire and distant memories flowed through his mind.

Chapter 36

Rex wasn't in the least tired and had no intention of finding a place to sleep just yet, not with all the activities taking place in the community, with shouts, screams and loud laughter. The Black Creek men and women were leaving and not quietly by any stretch of the imagination. It was chaos, as barrels were being rolled out of the grog shops, and loaded on to drays, a lot that they had stolen from the local community.

Standing in the shadow of a slab building, Rex saw the two men he had seen earlier talking in the undergrowth, behind the barracks. They were walking quite openly down the track leading out of the settlement, past the cesspits. He decided he wanted to hear what they were talking about on their walk, because the younger one was a colleague. He had discovered he had a gift of moving quietly some years ago, at night in Sunny Flat. He and his friends, when they were younger, caused problems for the older boys who were unmarried, by creeping up on them at times not appreciated! It had been a time to be able to run fast and not be identified!.

This was different because the raid on the settlement had been brutal and no one was safe. There were not many valuables in the settlement, now many had changed hands by force.

Rex wanted to know what was being discussed so earnestly as they strolled along the track. Moving quietly he managed to get within hearing distance, amongst other people who were also walking. He identified his colleague as Alf Stokes. At this part of the path another man led a horse up to the man who Rex had identified as Frank Black, who mounted the horse and told Alf to walk beside him, as they continued down the track.

"Alf, you've done a good job for me since the Closed Valley operation, it was a great pity you couldn't have saved my partner's life. Your recent work has been greatly appreciated, but the problem with a man who so readily betrays his colleagues, can't be trusted not to turn……on me for instance?" he was saying to Alf.

"I'd never do that, Mr. Black."

"No, and I'm not going to give you the chance to do it. Sorry Alf, I don't need you anymore."

Alf was shocked into complete silence, as he saw the gun pointed at him and heard the shot, and felt the sudden pain then nothing.

Mr. Black called to a couple of men who were obviously waiting for instructions, "Strip him, weigh him with chain and dump him in the cesspit, shovel in the soil, it stinks and it's time to fill it in."

Rex didn't move until the men had completed the task and vanished into the night. Even then he remained for a time until he felt completely alone and it was safe to crawl away. He laughed quietly saying to himself 'Weasel would now have an appropriate companion in his grave with Alf.'

Rex found a quiet stable which was unattended and went to sleep after an interesting night. No one disturbed him until the sun was well over the horizon. The owner kicked him awake and told him to get going or he'd feel the end of his boot again.

He went to Ma's tent and found men already there eating bowls of a dark soup with bits of meat in it.

"After you've eaten Rex, go and unlock your friends and send them to me for food," she said putting a bowl in front of him.

"Thank you Ma, they'll probably want to clean up a bit before coming here."

Chapter 37

Sam Hade drove his two-horse dray with a firm hand and a steady pace, having his elder son Andrew as a companion. In the dray was a long ladder. Sam had taken one look at the rope ladder and thought it looked unsafe for anyone of his size. He was horrified that his sons had used it in such a dangerous place without his knowledge and now they were happy to use it again. It would probably hold their weight, but he'd rather they used the ladder. Also in the tray were medical items, water, food, rope and a sling plus some added horse equipment. Shaun and Patrick were driving the second dray and Toby was riding his horse. They were still young enough to think of this job as an adventure, whereas Andrew and his Father knew there was a deadly side to it, a planned cruel death and Sam hoped they'd be in time to save lives.

Andrew had asked his father about the rope ladder which his three younger brothers had made last year. Sam began the story to take his mind away from what he might see at the mine shaft.

"Your brothers had gone for a ride to look at the old gold field on the eastern side of the mountain. Just inside the first row of trees they saw an old black man looking down into the shaft. Your brothers went and stood either side of him and looked down too."

"Are they never afraid?" Andrew asked.

"They have an ability to sum up a person instantly, they knew they were safe in the company of this Old Man," then he continued. "Being curious, the boys looked into the black hole and saw old bones sticking out of the sheer sides, until it was too dark to see them. They were able to communicate with each other and the Old Man told them the miners had dug through an ancient Burial Ground. He wanted to retrieve all the bones of his ancestors and re-bury them in a place of peace. The boys said they would help him and as you can imagine, they like anything new and exciting. Between them they made a rope ladder, like one they'd seen on a ship."

"I often wonder when I'm an old man, will I still have my three younger brothers!" Andrew mused.

"Try thinking about being their Father!"

"Hard for you and Mum?"

"Yes, we were relieved to see you all home at night, with scratches, torn clothes and bloody, but home. We also decided never to ask what you had been doing to get into that state, just as long as you came home." His Father continued, "They made the ladder out of rope, leather strips and sticks, and when I first saw it after it had been used with prayer! You're aware that Toby can climb like a monkey, followed closely by the other two boys, if the ladder had broken, they had the rope. They went down and collected all the bones for the Old Man. We never knew about it for some weeks. They were happy going riding each day, and coming home with the usual scratches, bits of dried blood on their clothes, as usual…"

"How did you find out?" Andrew asked.

"The Old Man came to visit me on the farm. I was sure I was on my own out in the paddock when he just arrived from among the trees. He has a presence, almost regal, I felt it the moment he came up to me. In his broken English, he told me I had good. happy boys as my sons. He said they were not afraid of him and he smiled. In a moment he continued, telling me that my boys were happy to go down into the shaft to get the bones. He stated something else that your Mother and I will always treasure, 'Dae live to great age, no worry.' Sam continued, "I only hope he's right, because between the four of you, you are sending your Mother and I grey before our time."

"What do you expect from your four sons, so much like the way you are, in all that you do!" Andrew laughed.

"I never went down a mine shaft on a highly questionable rope ladder for about fourteen feet."

"Only because you didn't need to go down a shaft. If you had, I've no doubt you would've found a more difficult way to do it."

"Andrew, mind your horses," his Father said.

"I am Dad."

*

The two drays made good time and as the sun rose above the eastern horizon, they passed the entrance to the valley. On the southern side of the mountain, Sam was always interested in the work Fred Hall was doing, he could see more trees had been removed, creating more grassland. They continued around the southern side and up the eastern tree line towards the old gold mine. A water course wound its way down a section of the mountain near the mine which dried up in the hot months.

"An old miner told me, the shaft was dug because gold was found on the surface of the ground. It was thought to have been uncovered by the rain," Sam explained.

"Did it produce much gold?"

"I don't think so, but it did bring up a lot of bones! The old miner added, strange things began to happen at that place, men began to leave it, we didn't know it was an ancient burial ground. Something happened, and all the remaining men left on the same day, they couldn't get away quick enough. I never discovered what had frightened the men."

As they neared the mine, Toby said, "Be careful where you walk, you don't want to slip into one of these holes, some are quite deep. Our one is just past the first line of trees."

Toby walked up to the top of the opening to the shaft, and called out, "Anyone awake?"

This was met by silence, not even the song of a bird, silence…

"I thought I heard a very weak sound, but it could have been an animal?" Shaun said.

Sam brought the dray up as close as he felt was safe to do and unhitched the two horses. Using the ropes and the sling he'd brought with him, he directed his sons in what he wanted done, in bringing a man up out of the shaft. The ladder was carefully put down the side of the shaft.

"How much room is there at the bottom of the shaft?" He asked Toby.

"It's fourteen feet deep and about six feet wide at the bottom. We didn't go right down on the ladder, it only went down twelve feet."

"I suppose you dropped down the last two feet?"

"Yes Dad, we had to get the bones for the Old Man."

Sam looked into the mine and checked his equipment, as he had seen in the army years ago.

"You go down carefully and see who is at the bottom of the shaft?" He asked Toby.

"There are three men down here, with Alex Pitt on the top of the other two men," Toby called out.

"Breathing?" His Father asked.

"Two are, except the man on the bottom, I think he's dead."

Toby returned to the surface and Shaun said quietly, "We seem to have got here in time to save the lives of two men, if only we'd known about it earlier."

"Shaun, it wouldn't have made any difference, the weight of two men falling on top of each other from fourteen feet, it's amazing that the second man's alive." Sam said.

Slowly the men were brought to the surface, and they recognised Tom Hunt and the dead man as one of his security men. Alex and Tom were unconscious and Sam directed Patrick to carefully pour some water into their mouths.

"Don't let them choke, just a tiny trickle."

Sam completed his rough examination on the ground beside the shaft.

"Tom has a broken leg, Alex has a broken arm and a dislocated shoulder. We'll put the shoulder back in now," Sam said, which he did assisted by his sons.

Alex and Tom were carefully put in one dray with Sam in with them and Andrew driving the two horses.

"This has to be a fast trip, on the smoothest track possible, Andrew," he instructed his son.

"Yes Dad, I know."

The other boys took the spare dray with all the equipment and Toby rode ahead to prepare his Mother and Jane, his sister, to have two beds ready.

"Shaun and Patrick are bringing the dead man in their dray," he told them.

"Who is it?" Jane asked.

"We aren't sure, we thought you could draw a picture of his face, before he's buried."

When the second dray arrived, Jane did the drawing of the man, like a portrait on the chance he had family somewhere. She had seen a dead person before this man, life on the frontier was an open one, people had accidents and died, it was a fact of life.

While the two men were unconscious, they were stripped of their clothes, washed and put into a nightgown. Tom's leg was put into splints and the arm of Alex, likewise, their other injuries were treated by Sam and his wife Elizabeth.

"I'd rather they stayed asleep a bit longer, but they need fluid and they'll need careful nursing. Where is John?"

"Here, Mr. Hade."

"Did you look at the dead man?"

"Yes, he's Jack, one of their security men."

"Does that mean there is another security man missing?"

"Yes and his name's Abe."

"Are you happy for us to bury Jack here on our Farm?"

"Yes, I can do the burial Service, if you would like me to do it?"

"Yes you can do it, we'll all attend, except my wife and Jane."

After the burial, Sam requested that everyone do a turn in watching the men.

"I don't want either man waking up alone in a strange house. Remember their last memory is being pushed down the open face of a mine shaft," he said.

"Do we tell them where they are?" Andrew asked.

"Yes of course, they'll know they're safe here."

"You have a job to do for the Old Man," Sam reminded Shaun, Toby and Patrick.

"We can go and do it, when the men wake up," Toby replied.

"You may have noticed a large pile of soil and stones on the top side of the shaft," Shaun explained.

"I did notice it, because it was in my way and I wondered who had been silly enough to put it so close to the opening."

"How were we to know our Father would be wanting to remove living bones from the shaft," Patrick said in their defense.

"There's more behind that pile of soil. We did it sometime ago, to be ready when the time came to fill it in," Toby added.

"Do you mean that there might be something more interesting to do, when the time comes for you to fill it in, and you'd want to do it in a couple of days," their Father suggested.

"Yes Dad, that's exactly what we thought at the time."

"The Old Man?"

"He knows we'll fill in the shaft for him," Toby replied cheerfully.

Alex was the first to wake up, becoming instantly aware of the discomfort in his left arm. He remembered falling and landing on Tom, who had been pushed down before him. Turning his head slightly he saw another bed, and a man on it, with Toby sitting beside him.

"How long?" He croaked, turning his head again, he looked at Shaun whom he recognised.

"A few hours Mr. Pitt."

"Other man, Tom?"

"Yes, Mr. Pitt. You must have a drink."

Shaun lifted Alex's head gently and gave him some water which had been sweetened.

"I'll get Dad," he said.

Sam came into the room and said, "Alex, sleep if you can, your body and mind have endured a nasty experience, it will take time to heal."

Alex heard the words and drifted back to sleep. Patrick changed places with Toby, who wanted to go and check on the horses, and secure the rope ladder away from Andrew, back to its secret place in the stables.

Tom woke up half an hour later than Alex and was instantly aware of his broken leg in splints. His last memory was of falling on to Jack who never uttered a word as he was pushed down first. It had been really awful at the top of the shaft, when they'd been brought to it by a group of men, one of whom was his own security guard, Abe. Jack called him every name he could bring himself to say at his betrayal. Tom remembered it was Abe who pushed Jack into the shaft and he fell silently. This betrayal of himself had really hurt his pride in his choice of men and wondered if he could ever trust his security men again.

"Who are you?" he turned his head and asked in a voice which didn't sound like his own.

"Shaun Hade, Mr. Hunt. Can I help you to some sweetened water?"

Shaun gently lifted his head and he drank a small quantity of it. He asked the same kind of questions which Alex had done, then returned to sleep.

A week later, Abe was looking forward to meeting the man who had employed him to betray Tom Hunt. He didn't look upon it as a betrayal in so many words, more of an investment in his future. Tom Hunt had employed him to protect his goods. Another man had employed him to supply information, which led to the mine shaft. He hadn't countered on being told to push them both down it. That hadn't felt right, but Jack made it easier by cursing him. He enjoyed shutting him up, but the look Tom Hunt gave him silently, when his turn came, was strange and he was unable to interpret it. The policeman had also looked at him in silence, with an expression he'd been unable to identify, perhaps he would one day.

The man rode up to the meeting place, stayed on his horse and asked, "Are Alex Pitt, Tom Hunt and Jack now in the shaft?"

"Yes Mr. Black."

"Is it filled in?"

"Yes, it's filled in," Abe replied, although he didn't know who'd filled in the shaft.

"Good, this is your pay," He said raising the gun he'd hidden on his saddle and shot him without mercy.

An expression flashed across Abe's face, at last understanding the expressions on the faces of the two men he had killed.

"You poor fool, as if I'd waste good money on you," he heard Frank Black say in a fading tone and riding away without a care in the world.

Chapter 38

As Rex left Ma's food tent and walked towards the barracks, he was delighted to see a dray coming towards him loaded with saddles, horse equipment and best of all, police uniforms from the Cameron farm. It didn't take him long to have a good wash and put on his uniform. Once satisfied with himself, he walked down to the lock-up, removed the iron bar and opened the door.

"Right you're free, don't do it again!"

"Thank you Mr. Howard, have the Black Creek men left us?" His Sergeant greeted him with a question.

"Yes Sergeant, they packed up and left us during the night."

"I've never known until now how good fresh air feels at this hour of the morning," He said, looking pleased, then adding with a smile, "This feeling is no reflection on the present gentlemen surrounding me, who have spent time in our lock-up."

As the Sergeant walked away up towards his home, Ian was still feeling irritated with Rex, "You could've opened the door last night."

"They were still here when I found a place to sleep," Rex replied in a slightly irritated tone.

Ian had no intention of being grateful to Rex for letting them him out of the stinking lock-up.

"It's past sunrise, why are you letting us out this late in the morning?" he growled.

"Ma asked me to let you out now and she'll have hot food for you," Rex replied looking at his other colleagues. He turned to face Ian and said, "If you'd been in another cell, I would've been inclined to leave the grumpy old men in until at least midday."

"Come on to the food tent, we're fortunate he let us out at all!" Bill said, and seeing Ian's expression, tugged his arm.

"He irritates me," Ian smiled at his friend.

"Now you know what it feels like, having Bill Todd near me," Charley, who on hearing these words, said to Ian.

"I've been locked up with Bill, Charley and Ian in open warfare, only the Sergeant kept the peace. Where is Nick Rose?" Harry White mused out loud.

"He went with John and Willie," Rex answered.

They all walked up to their barracks. Bill and Ian saw their uniforms, with their saddles and equipment outside the door of the building.

"When did these arrive here?" Bill asked Rex.

"At the same time as I came from Ma's tent."

"That is why you washed and changed?"

"Yes Bill, I could hardly wait to get out of those stinking clothes."

"You get used to smelly clothes," Bill said gruffly.

"That might be so but not the constant insects which bite."

"Has it been bad in the community for the last couple of days?" Bill asked.

"Yes, for the people trying to improve their way of living, this raid has been brutal."

"Let's have a wash like Rex has, get into our uniforms and go to Ma's for a hot meal," Bill turned to Ian and suggested.

Rex went into the barracks to find his own trunk. The Black Creek men had turned the whole room upside down, emptied all the trunks and taken what had caught their eye. All the bunks were pulled apart and the straw spread over everything, it was total chaos. They would need to get fresh straw to create their bunks. There was no doubt the clean-up would take all day just to get the basic part into working order. During this process for the whole community, Ma's food tent became the focal meeting place of the police, and members of the community, who now struggled to get back to normal.

There were fights in the settlement with those who had sided with the invaders to get even on neighbours over petty slights. Now some of these people packed up and left, with checks being made on their goods, making sure they were only taking what belonged to them. The anger was real in the community and the police were expected to keep the peace, as well as sorting out their own barracks.

*

Ian saw Sergeant Green walk towards his office and called out, "Have you been inside it yet, Sergeant?"

"No, I presume it's a total mess."

"Yes it is, papers scattered everywhere."

"Are the two stools in front of my desk still in their right place?" His Sergeant asked.

"They haven't been touched at all," Ian replied, noticing a relieved smile settling on his Sergeant's face.

On the late afternoon of the second day, Nick Rose arrived with the Green Hills police. They were greeted with relief as it allowed the local police to continue sorting out the barracks and stables, making a list for replacements of horse equipment.

"How did you know the Black Creek men were coming?" The Sergeant asked Nick.

Nick explained what Willie had suspected but didn't have any proof and asked him to ride to Green Hills to request help. Late in the afternoon the Sergeant received a message informing him that Tom Hunt was missing, his dray had been found wrecked, all his goods stolen and there was no sign of his security men.

In the early evening another message to say, "The men have begun to enter the top part of the ranges in groups."

It came from Inspector Jason Stone, who was working undercover at the grog shanty outside Deep Glen. The Sergeant composed a second message attached to the one he had received, and sent it down south, by the same messenger after he'd had a meal and was given more rations for his trip.

The Sergeant called a meeting of his police to review the last few days, also to question Rex because he was the only policeman not captured and put under lock and key.

Rex told his story and what he'd witnessed on the evening the raiders had left the community.

"We only have your word for Alf's death," Ian said, still irritated with Rex.

"He isn't going anywhere!" Rex replied.

"When Mr. Percy and Mr. Howard have finished talking, we will proceed," the Sergeant sighed and said.

"A point needed clarification Sergeant," Ian spoke firmly.

"It wouldn't have needed to be clarified Mr. Percy, if you'd been paying attention to Mr. Howard's story of the cesspit."

"I was listening Sergeant. It just seemed to me that Mr. Howard was exaggerating the event."

The Sergeant, though irritated with Ian, smiled and said, "Mr. Percy you can accompany Mr. Rush and the men he chooses to dig up the cesspit. I will expect you to return to me with the clarification of Mr. Howard's story. No doubt you can identify Mr. Stokes and Weasel?"

"Yes Sergeant"

No one smiled, though they all enjoyed Ian's discomfort, because he had been difficult from the moment he was locked up but it had been a difficult for all of the men. Ian was normally an easy-going man and no one could understand his current behaviour. Bill had done his best to keep tempers under control. No one knew what Rex had done to bring out the worst in Ian Percy. Bill could have told them, but it wouldn't have helped the situation. Rex was young and happy and it had irritated Ian, particularly on a night, in a certain tent in the community.

A couple of hours later Ian returned to the office with Charley, to confirm the story of the two bodies, as Rex had explained.

"Are they at the cemetery now?" The Sergeant asked, thanking the men.

"Yes Sergeant, and being buried," Charley replied.

"That will be all gentlemen."

Soon afterward they'd left he was surprised to see his two nephews walk into his office. Greeting Andrew and Patrick Hade, he learnt that they had used the mares owned by Mr. Cameron to come to Hill Top and put them in the police stables They explained the reason for this ride and John Hale's request for a dray with two horses. They also asked that they be given two police horses to take back for the two police at the Hade farm. Andrew and Patrick stayed at the barracks for the night and ate a meal at Ma's food tent. As with everyone, Ma was deeply shocked that Alex had been put down the mine shaft. In the barracks the boys re-told the story with additions, which they hadn't told their Uncle and Patrick talked about their earlier experience at the gold mine. Ian was interested in the Old Man and he told Patrick and Andrew about his and Bill's encounter with this extraordinary man.

Andrew and Patrick were given police horses and equipment for the now stranded policemen at the Hade farm. They rode out of the police yard at sunrise for home.

Chapter 39

Within a few days both Tom and Alex were making good progress and learning to cope with their broken limbs but the shock of being pushed down a mine shaft was another matter.

"This experience may take years to recover from showing itself in nightmares. I can't tell you how, only that they seem to have a cycle of their own," Sam suggested.

Both men were enormously grateful to the Hade family, but the desire to go home was equally strong, to be amongst their own kind, whether it was the barracks or the Victoria Inn. Willie also wanted to return to the barracks. It was with considerable anticipation that they waited for Andrew and Patrick to return from Hill Top, with the news that Charley Rush and Andrew Willow were following in a dray.

"Am I going with Alex?" Tom asked.

"Yes Mr. Hunt, a message was sent to your brother, to tell him that Mr. Rush will meet him at the cross tracks coming from the west to join the south one," Andrew replied to which Tom smiled.

Alex was aware that a dray was slower than the horse's walk, so it was no surprise to him that Charley and Andrew Willow arrived a few days after the others had come home. They camped down beside the creek as usual, it was almost like being with the family, because the four young men visited frequently with meat and other nice things to eat.

The planned return was for John, Willie and Andrew to ride the horses. Sam Hade made a suggestion as to how it would be easier to fit Alex and Tom in the dray. Tom had no choice in this matter. As a way of helping he told the men a few stories of how he'd seen men in similar situations having to travel. In doing so Tom began to feel fortunate in being with the police!

They left the farm the next day and the men on their horses rode at the same pace as the dray. It took two days to reach the cross-tracks, which was a new camp site a short distance from the old one. In wet weather it had become boggy and nearly all drays became stuck, which was the problem being close to water. The new one was still within walking distance of the creek on a rise with some large rocks. Both Alex and Tom were relieved each night to get out of the dray. Even though Tom had a crutch and a stick to walk, he needed help to get out of the two wheeled dray, it needed to be kept steady and John was always ready to assist him. Charley did the same for Alex, while the other men saw to the horses, with Andrew doing most of the work.

Dick Hunt arrived the next day driving two horses in the two-wheeled dray and Bob Pringle riding his horse. They were the only people at this site until the late afternoon, when Andrew said, "There are four men on horses coming this way."

As the four men came closer, Tom said quietly, "We're in for it now, the man in the middle is William Knox, the second in command to Frank Black. He was present when we were pushed into the mine."

Instantly guns were loaded and put within reach, Alex and Tom moved closer to the rocks for protection. Bob and John stayed close to the men. Tom and Alex could only lie still and watch the riders as they drew close to the camp, and as yet they hadn't seen the two wounded men.

"Can we boil a quart-pot?" William Knox asked, recognising this was a police gathering.

"No, move on," Charley replied in an unfriendly tone.

Knox turned suddenly and saw Alex and Tom and ground out in a voice as cold as ice, "F— hell you're alive, you're meant to be dead and buried, but you soon will be!"

He looked at the police and saw the guns near their fingertips. No one moved as Charley saw Knox weighing up his chances of survival if a shot was fired. Knox knew his life was in danger from Frank Black if he discovered those bastards Pitt and Hunt were still alive. They were protected for the moment and were a long way from the barracks.

"What's it to be Knox?" Charley asked.

Knox began to back away across the uneven ground, step by step, his hand close to his gun. Suddenly without any warning his boot slipped, his hand clasped hard on his gun and a shot was fired accidently. Instantly his three companions fired into the group of police. In seconds two groups of men were taking cover, as bullets flew in both directions followed by silence. The police had suffered no serious wounds. Tom had a bullet graze his shoulder, and a bullet went through Andrew's boot missing his leg. Two of the men with Knox were dead and the other nursing a wound. Knox was unscathed and kept moving backwards, being watched by Charley as if he was a dangerous reptile. Knox wondered why they hadn't shot him when they had the chance.

"Have you had enough Knox?" Charley asked, adding, "I can end your miserable life now."

Knox was unaware that one of the policemen had moved around the rocks, and had come up behind him, as Charley had been talking. He suddenly felt a gun barrel pressing into his back and heard the command, "Drop your gun Knox."

Instantly his wounded friend dropped his gun too.

"We want some answers," Charley said.

Willie had kept his gun on the wounded man, with the result that Knox wasn't warned of his danger.

"Why did you put those two men down the mine shaft?" Charley enquired.

"Orders from the Boss. You can't keep me here, I'm a policeman the same as you are."

"I'm not a murdering bastard like you, nor do I push colleagues down a mine shaft, however much they might deserve it."

"Doesn't matter Rush your time is almost over. In a few weeks we'll clean out the ranges of Sefton and his brood. The boss knows where they're hiding and he'll flush them out. Then you'll find out who's the real Boss."

"In the meantime get those bodies out of our sight," Charley said.

Knox and his wounded friend tied the bodies to their horses and rode away in an easterly direction.

"What's the betting Charley, they will drop the bodies somewhere, and ride on?" Willie asked.

"I'm not betting against you Willie, it's what I'd do if I was Knox."

"Those two men we shot were they police?" Dick enquired.

"No, nor was the wounded one, those men do dirty work for Knox," Alex replied.

"Knox will give me nightmares, he really is an evil man," Tom said quietly.

"Anyone near Frank Black has been contaminated beyond redemption in our opinion," Bob mused.

Early in the next morning Dick helped his brother into the dray and Bob mounted his horse. He and Dick would do a number of hours on the dray. The job of riding the horse was to keep an eye out for trouble on their way down to Sunny Flat.

Charley had no intention of handing the reins of the dray horses to anyone else but himself.

It was a slow ride surrounded by his colleagues, who took the strain away from checking the countryside for danger. Knox wasn't the kind of man to give up, not with a ruthless man like Black behind him. Charley fully expected another attempt on the life of Alex.

"I want a couple of you men to wear coats tomorrow," he said at the next camp.

"It's a cold wind blowing, but we don't need coats, what have you in mind Charley?" Willie enquired.

"Willie, I'm expecting another attack, so I want Alex on a horse tomorrow, with a coat covering his broken arm."

"Whose horse?"

"Andy's horse."

"Where am I going to be, Charley?" Andrew Willow asked.

"As far as you can, get under the seat of the dray, we'll create a dummy in police uniform, who will sit in the back of the dray, to be the target."

"Charley, are you sure Knox will make another attack on Alex?" John enquired.

"Yes I'm sure, because with Alex and Tom alive, he knows he could be killed by Black. He'll make one more effort as we're still a long way from safety. If he succeeds, Alex will disappear forever.

The next day Alex was mounted on a gentle horse and disguised, as much as possible, after giving up his seat in the dray, to a police dummy, which was really quite well done and from a distance looked real. As usual, they rode in a tight formation into the hills keeping their hands firmly on the reins of their horses and feeling for the least form of trouble. This was to keep their mounts from acting independently if they became uneasy.

"I feel we're under observation so hold your horses firmly and be alert As you can see ahead, we're about to pass a place where an attack could take place," Charley said.

They passed a place which had undergrowth on either side of the track and a high hill on one side. There was no attack. The morning vanished and in the early afternoon, the shots came rapidly from above them. The dummy took a number of hits, the force of the hits caused it to fall over and lie flat on the bottom of the dray. Charley instantly pulled up the horses and hurried to the back of the dray, giving every indication that they had a dead man in the dray.

Their last camp was a quiet one, again feigning mourning, before setting out early the next day on the last leg of their journey to Hill Top. The dummy was wrapped up and laid flat in the back of the dray.

They arrived safely at the barracks and Alex had to be helped to dismount. Standing on the ground near the stables, Alex complimented Charley for having an excellent idea, which saved his life a second time.

Chapter 40

Sergeant Green called a meeting of the police on the late afternoon of Alex being returned to the barracks.

"I have received a request from Red Bryant, that all the police who were stockmen in their civilian lives report to him at "Red's Land" as soon as they can ride down to his property. He also requested another farrier with blacksmith experience, which means you, Mr. Howard."

"I trained as a farrier," Rex explained.

"I've been expecting this call for some days. You have all been aware of a certain police operation and this is part of it. Mr. White, Mr. Rose and Mr. Howard will leave here early tomorrow morning. Mr. Percy and Mr. Todd will leave the next day. Remember you will have two camps, so take enough rations as it's a three-day ride," he continued.

"Always take spare bullets, tell the others and look out for trouble, that area isn't safe at the present time," Charley said, pulling Harry aside.

"Charley, is it the Black Creek men?" Nick enquired.

"Yes Nick, we were fortunate to get Alex back alive, so be careful."

Taking Charley's advice the three men took extra bullets and rations, leaving at sunrise the next morning. Nick knew the way to "Red's Land" as he had driven a herd of cattle to the property before joining the police. The first day was uneventful, as they talked and became better acquainted with each other. Long hours in the saddle caused deeper discussions than was possible in the barracks. In growing knowledge were the seeds of enjoyment of each other's company, which could last for a lifetime.

On the second day they left camp before the sun rose over the eastern hills, continuing to ride south. In the mid-morning they heard gunshots and pulled up their mounts

"Someone is firing at that slab hut. You can just see it through the trees, west of us," . Harry said.

"It isn't just one man, there's more than one, they've surrounded the hut," Rex commented.

"Do we split up, or charge as a group?" Nick asked.

"I see three horses in the yard near a dray, if we move closer, we can fire above the men's heads, our action could be all that is required to stop them shooting at the hut," Rex said.

"Nick, you aim for a leg and we'll fire over their heads as a warning," Harry agreed, saying.

The three police rode straight at the hut, Those attacking the people in the hut didn't hear the approach of the horses until the last moment, when one of the men felt a bullet. The others looked east and were shocked to see the police, and not wishing to answer any questions they turned and rode away in haste through the trees.

The wooden door opened carefully and a man emerged, seeing the police, he smiled and looked enormously relieved and strode forward, with his hand outstretched to each of the police, who had dismounted.

"I'm Dick Hunt, you've come past here at the right time. We couldn't have held them off much longer."

"If you're Dick Hunt, then your brother is Tom who has a broken leg?"

"Yes, you're correct, he's inside the hut with Bob Pringle."

"We were told about you by Charley Rush, who thought you could be in trouble, after leaving the cross-track camp," Nick continued.

"Alex got home safely, after Charley made a dummy and put it on the back of the dray. Alex was put on a horse wearing a coat as did his colleagues," Harry added.

"They shot up the dummy!" Rex chipped in.

"I think you'd better come along with us to "Red's Land", if you get caught again someone will have to dig graves," Nick suggested.

"Tom doesn't want to get any closer to a grave than he did in that mine shaft, so we're happy to go along with you," Dick answered.

"How did they catch you?" Harry asked.

"Bob rode ahead of our dray and saw a group of men checking everyone walking south on the track. We were unable to get past them so Bob rode either side of the track to find somewhere we could defend and found this abandoned hut, close to the track. We only had enough time to put the horses in the yard when they found us."

"I told Dick that three Hill Top police would be riding down the track about this time, and would certainly investigate shooting near it," Bob added.

"How did you know we would be riding down here?" Rex enquired.

"Coming down behind you, the day after you left your barracks, will be Bill and Ian," Bob smiled and gave Rex another piece of knowledge.

The three young police looked surprised and decided not to make any other enquiries, As Rex helped Dick put the two horses back into the shafts of the dray, he explained about Bob Pringle saying, "Special police officer."

They continued south for the remainder of the day, choosing a campsite in an open area near water for the horses. Tom obviously hated being an invalid and needed help for just about everything he needed to do. At last he settled down beside the fire, leaning against a log with the other men, who had gathered around to watch the quart-pots beginning to boil. Bob had been carrying a pot and tin bowls in the dray, plus the ingredients for making a hot stew.

"Bob married our sister Betsy and they run a large dining room in our Mother's Victoria Inn in Sunny Flat. Between the two of them their meals have become quite famous," Dick explained.

"Bob you can cook for us anytime!" Harry said after he had eaten his meal.

When the meal had been completed the men sat around the fire in the quiet of the night.

"Tom, do you want to talk about how your leg got broken?" Rex asked.

"You don't have to talk about that awful experience Tom, if you don't want to," Dick said, immediately going on the defensive.

Tom put his arm along his brother's shoulder and replied quietly, as Dick glared at Rex.

"It's better to have it out in the open than tied up inside," Tom answered, looking across the fire at Rex.

"I suppose it's easier talking to you Rex, because we've known you since our family moved to Sunny Flat. Later you can answer questions from Nick and Harry who have never been to our settlement."

"Are you suggesting I explain what you leave out of your story?"

"Yes please Rex."

Tom began to talk about the long trip returning to Sunny Flat, after making a delivery in the north to a property, on the edge of a new settlement, as yet unnamed.

"On a long trip like this one, I have to take at least two security men, you're well aware of the constant dangers of thieves out on the tracks through the bush. On this trip I took my most trusted men to guard my dray, Jack Lessing and Abe Kane," he said.

Tom went on to explain that he had bought goods for Jason's shop and they were on their way home .

He stopped talking for a moment and said, "I want to talk about my two security men. They were the kind of men who looked as if they could use clubs if they were attacked by thieves. Jack had been with me for two years, he had no family and made his home in our community at Sunny Flat, he proved to be a loyal and honest man, many times."

"And Abe Kane?" Rex enquired

"He would never have fitted into Sunny Flat, having no ability to build anything, I kept him on as a guard thinking that on our journeys he might find somewhere he'd like to stay."

"How did Jack get on with him?" Rex asked.

"He tolerated him and made a supreme effort not to punch him for being stupid and thoughtless on lots of occasions."

"And the betrayal?" Rex said quietly.

"Jack refused to leave me when he was given the chance to. It happened at a campsite, Abe had been drinking and in the morning, Jack saw two pairs of hobbles still on the dray. He also saw the spokes of the dray had been disconnected, so it couldn't be used at all. Jack was furious and walked towards Abe, who drew a gun and said to us, 'This is the end of your line.' To me he said cheerfully, 'You buy and sell and now I've sold you!' He laughed and Jack asked, 'How much did you get for me?' 'Nothing, it was two for the price of one, you had your chance to walk away.'"

"What happened?" Rex prompted.

"We waited until William Knox arrived with another dray and two of his men, who unloaded my dray and put it all on their dray. Jack was given another opportunity to leave and refused the offer."

"Those men never leave any witnesses, if he'd walked away he would've been shot in the back," Rex said thoughtfully.

"Did you have to put that thought into my mind?" Tom said.

"Yes, because you would've come to that conclusion yourself in time. I'm not doubting his loyalty, remember his background, he would've known what was in their minds. Being with you was the best choice he had at that moment. Jack did save your life, regardless of his motives at the bottom of the shaft."

There was silence around the fire, no one moved as Tom continued, "We were taken to the slab hut after a long walk and met Alex Pitt. He'd been in there for a couple of days. We spent a short time together before they came and put us in a dray for the long ride out to Black Mountain."

"What do you remember about that trip?" Rex asked.

"Alex was quite calm and talked quietly with Jack. I do remember he made Jack laugh, which irritated our guard. It was a peaceful ride through the lovely countryside for most of the way. Once the mountain came into our sight, I wondered what they were going to do with us." Tom continued, "Jack whispered, 'We're going to a haunted place'. William Knox taunted us as we walked from the dray to the edge of the shaft. Now we knew our destination, Jack was in front of us and the moment he reached the edge of the pit, Abe gave him a push and laughed. As Jack fell he cried out, 'You bastard Abe, I'll see you in hell.' They didn't waste time, I was the next to be pushed by Abe. I remember falling into a black hole, I have no memory of landing on Jack. I didn't regain consciousness until I woke up in the Hade Family home."

"Tom, you might be interested to know, before we left Hill Top, a message was received that a body had been found, which was believed to be Abe Kane, he'd been shot. They don't leave any witnesses ever." Rex added.

The next day they broke camp at the usual time.

"Tom had a good night, telling his story has quietened his mind, though I suspect he will have many nightmares about falling into that mine shaft," Bob quietly informed Dick.

"I thought he looked a lot better last night after Rex had kept him talking," Dick replied.

They had a few words to say about Rex!.

It was a long slow ride to "Red's Land", arriving in middle twilight. Red and Mary took charge of Tom, while Bob went to help in the kitchen area and the three police stockmen were made welcome.

Chapter 41

"**I** want you to accompany Dick to Sunny Flat, leaving before sunrise tomorrow morning. Your two colleagues will go with you on the first day. Please return here as soon as you can after seeing Tom safely delivered to Sunny Flat," Red told Rex after introductions.

"Yes Mr. Bryant."

"I'm Red, not Mr. Bryant or you'll be in trouble!"

"The first night's camp?" Rex enquired.

"It will be a cattle camp, ask for Victor Gill, on your return trip you will meet up with him again."

Dick looked a lot more cheerful after a long talk with Red. Rex saw him have a quiet word with his brother and they both smiled. Bob noticed Rex observing both Tom and Dick and explained to him, "Red has told him what he expects to happen in the ranges on the next few days, but I can't add anything else."

"It's enough to know that something is happening Bob."

They left the next morning as requested and in the late afternoon, Rex was amazed to see a large herd of cattle, probably over a thousand in number. Victor was in the main camp and explained, "This herd is a combination of eight brands, all different owners combining for the operation."

Rex told him of the instructions he had received from Red.

"I presume you know cattle walk at a slow pace, stopping to eat and drink if there is water available. I expect you will arrive the day after tomorrow," Victor explained.

"Where do you expect to be in two days?"

"Probably just about to enter the ranges, I want you back in time for the final planning session."

Riding around the herd to see if he knew any of the stockmen, he was pleased to find two men he had known at Sunny Flat. They were both the sons of squatters, Allan Waters and Tony Bolt. He soon discovered that they were excited to be part of this operation organized by Red, though they were unaware of exactly what it entailed. Their fathers had told them, 'Play your part, obey Red.'

"My father told me it's a vital operation for the welfare of our land." Allan said to Rex.

"My father told me the same line as Allan's father told him," Tony added. Tony had persisted in asking questions, until his father became irritated and said sternly, 'It's a secret, so just do it Tony.'

Rex had always enjoyed their company but was unable to answer Tony's or Allan's questions in a satisfactory manner, other than to say quietly, "It has something to do with a man who can take land away from squatters, who are the sons of convicts or closely related to them."

"Is it to stop him from doing it?" Tony asked.

"Yes Tony."

"Why couldn't Dad tell me?"

"Would you Tony tell anyone, even your own son?" Rex replied.

"No. It's a secret."

Rex turned to Allan and asked, "What are you thinking?"

"Do you know who has been blackmailed into doing something against their will?"

"I can't talk about it Allan, but this operation, in part, has stemmed from it."

"How long does it take for people to forget a convict connection?" Tony commented.

"That's why it is a secret Tony, always." Allan answered his friend.

Rex spent the night camp with his friends. In the morning they left the cattle camp before sunrise. Tom was more cheerful on this second part of the trip with Bob driving the dray. It was Dick's turn on his horse and he rode alongside Rex for several hours. Before it was his turn again to drive the dray. Rex was relieved he wasn't expected to drive it! They arrived in Sunny Flat in the late afternoon. There were greetings all round at the Victoria Inn when they had driven into the backyard of the Inn. As soon as Rex could escape, he went to see his parents, on his way previous girlfriends admired him in his police uniform.

"Much more of this Rex and I'll dump you in the creek!!" His younger brother, who was a witness to one of these encounters, said.

"As if you could Bertie!!" Rex laughed and gave his brother a hug.

"I'll have my friends to help me!"

Bertie was proud of his elder brother, but as usual never let on in any way his feelings for him. They had a strong bond in common, they both loved horses, any horse not tied up or in a yard or paddock, was inclined to follow them!. When they were young boys, their parents were forever trying to find the owners of horses, which had followed them home. As a result this house was well known in Sunny Flat.

In the early morning at dawn Rex walked to the stable to saddle his horse. He wasn't surprised to find his brother Bertie already in the stable. As Rex entered he saw the saddlecloth already across the back of his horse. He lifted the saddle up easily and Bertie began to do up the girth strap. Later he checked it but not in front of his brother. Bertie was a younger version of Rex and would be equally as handsome. They had a few words to each other, a hug and Rex mounted and with a last wave of his hand rode out of the yard, into the darkness of the early day in a northerly direction.

He kept up a steady pace and reached the tail end of the cattle herd in early twilight, to be greeted by Tony and Allan, who escorted him to the main camp, while other men took over the watch on the southern side for the next three hours. Keeping the herd intact, men took turns in the night watch as the cattle settled down for the night.

The meeting took place while the men were eating the evening meal and it concerned Tony, Allan, Harry and Nick.

"Red asked me to tell you about your place in the current operation. The cattle will be going up beside the river in the ranges. Your job will be to turn the leaders of the stock into a valley, just past the valley where Red lives, then down the long valley out into the open country. Six stockmen will be waiting for the herd to emerge and take them in hand," Victor explained. "Any questions?" he asked.

"Nick and I, do we go south too?" Harry enquired.

"No. You proceed to "Red's Land" to await instructions."

Victor handed a piece of paper to Tony, showing hills, valleys and places the cattle could go without careful attention.

"This is obviously a well-planned operation," Tony remarked.

"You'd be amazed at the amount of work which has gone into it," Victor smiled and said.

"What do I do?" Rex asked.

"Red wants you to go to this hill," Victor explained.

He pointed to a hill overlooking a valley on the paper being held by Tony. It showed a large camp of men in the valley below.

"These are men who will need watching. You'll be joined by Ian Percy and Bill Todd," he explained, adding ""It's an important position to watch and report."

It was quite obvious from the expression on Rex's face that he didn't like this posting but there was no question of not obeying Red's command. Rex left the camp at dawn with the four other young men, riding north to their appointed positions, while the herd moved slowly into the ranges.

Rex met up with Ian and Bill on their way to the appointed hill. They rode in silence until Bill asked, "We heard you had an interesting time going south, a couple of days ago."

Rex was happy to talk about that trip, as they slowly climbed the appointed hill, through thick undergrowth, clumps of trees and around deep gullies, following as usual animal tracks the whole way to the top. Ian chose a campsite surrounded by trees. It was a good place as they could look down into the valley, without being seen. It was slowly filling up with tents and men. The river was low with the result that men were camped on both sides of it, a narrow rough type of valley, as Bill and Ian remembered when they rode through it a couple of years ago. The horses were yarded up all together below the tall hill where the police had their camp.

Rex had used his spare time on the hill by examining the animal tracks leading to the valley below. They were steep in sections, but otherwise a long walk. His job was to carry messages between the hills and men. On his third night in early twilight, he handed a message to Bill, who read it and said to Ian

"It's tonight, Frank Black has entered the valley below."

"What's to happen tonight?" Rex enquired and Ian told him.

Bill and Ian were as usual wrapped up in themselves, and Rex thought, 'They won't miss me'.

He had a pair of dark trousers in his swag so changed out of his police pantaloons, and wasting no time, he hurried down the animal tracks to the base of the hill. Moving quietly and keeping to the shadows, he crept to where the horses were enclosed. The horses watched him undoing the western end of their enclosure, he moved amongst them undoing hobbles, also a young mare tied to the fence, checking that they were all free. He crept out again, keeping to the shadows, he took hold of the horse's mane and began to creep back up the hill. After a short distance he was able to take his hand away from the mane, looking back he saw they were all following him up the hill, a long line of beautiful horses.

Up on the hill Bill had gone looking for Rex and went to his swag and saw the police white pantaloons tossed to one side as if Rex was in a hurry. Bill didn't call Ian, instead went looking for Rex. At the edge of the hill he looked down in sheer surprise and wonder, It was a sight he would remember all his life. A man leading a long line of horses in all colours, climbing slowly upwards. Bill quietly called Ian to come to him. They both looked down to see this rare sight of at least sixty horses winding their way upwards.

"Where do you think he's taking the horses?" Ian asked.

"To safety, you know he loves horses."

"I do know it. He walks into the horse paddock, and they all run up to him. He doesn't have to run after them as we do."

They stood quietly and watched this sight which touched their souls.

"Rex can be a difficult young policeman, but his love of horses is a rare gift, as they love him too. It was very dangerous for him to go down into that camp of men." Bill said, expressing his thoughts

"I'd like to give him a lecture about it, but he'd just look at me, the way he does at times. It wouldn't make a scrap of difference to his thinking of saving the lives of those horses," Ian said.

An hour later after they'd seen him cross the hill and walk down towards the next valley, Rex stood to one side. The mare stopped beside him for a moment and he indicated to her to go downwards. The others followed and the last one was the young mare, he gave her a hug, she tossed her head and gently nudged him before following the older ones down the hill.

Rex returned to his swag and changed clothes, before going to the fire to see if there was enough water in his quart-pot to make tea, he was surprised to see Bill and Ian still at the fire.

"It was risky, you could've been caught." Bill said to Rex.

"Unlikely Bill, I'm accustomed to moving quietly in the undergrowth and the horses would never have given any indication of my being amongst them. In fact, I've even experienced a time when they've closed ranks around me, when they thought I was in danger."

"I think it was a brave act to go down that hill to save the horses, have you let anyone know of their existence?" Bill said quietly.

"Yes I saw one of the security men and told him about the horses."

"What did he say to you?" Ian enquired.

"Young idiot!" Rex grinned and replied. "He also told me that Inspector Jason Stone, who sent that message to you, also said something which was meaningless to me."

"What is it?" Ian asked.

"Red has an ancient friend who is helping him tonight."

Rex, who was watching their faces, saw instant understanding as Ian said, "I'm not surprised, Red is one of the most cunning men I've ever met, he doesn't leave anything to chance."

"No horse deserves to die this way tonight," He said looking at Rex.

Chapter 42

It heard the faint call to wake up, it didn't want to leave its dream world. Still the call came, insistent that it wake up, the call had penetrated through unknown numbers of centuries, nothing seemed to stop the call to wake up.

It didn't want to wake up, it had woken up in the early times, but not for eons, ages without number. It' had seen the changes in its world, animals like himself had vanished. There were new ones which lacked the size of its family.

No. He didn't want to wake up, the call was relentless in its demand to wake up. In its time it had reigned supreme and not at the beck and call on inferior animals. The call was ceaseless in its demand to wake up.

It remembered that it had seen itself as a reflection in the swamp water, it had been amazed at how handsome it was when it was young. A strong head, a mouth filled with flattened serrated teeth, powerful jaws, capable of bending outwards in the middle, to be able to get a firm grip on its prey. It had powerful forelimbs, heavily muscled, ending in three powerful fingers of grasping hands, with enormous claws. Now it was a mere shadow of its former glorious self. The call to wake up was relentless.

The call was now so strong, it felt itself being dragged through the mists of layers of time to an unfamiliar world. Where even in a shadowed existence, it couldn't sense any of its own kind. It did sense fear, which it did think was quite normal, it had arrived. It was curious, something was feeling afraid of it and it was only a shadow

It was a fear of the unknown, surely its kind were not unknown. It moved as the spirit of a great beast down the valley, with strange trees, it saw a strange creature on four stumpy legs and an unprotected soft skin. Amazing as it glided forward and looked down at this strange beast. For a brief time it was unaware of the presence of the Master of the World. This all changed when it sensed a claw tracing a line down the side of its body, it moved suddenly. It thought that the beast would've made a tasty meal, not much of it, two would be better. The irritating call had stopped, a merciful silence as it dropped back down through eons of time.

Chapter 43

The bull was of an advanced age, or at least this is how he saw himself. He had lots of cows to keep an eye on their activities. His other eye was kept on the younger bulls, they had learned the hard way that his long sharp horns could hurt the unwary. He knew how to protect his own territory and his cows within it.

They were all together in this valley, not only his herd of cows, but other bulls and their cows, lots of them. The night was quiet and all the animals were settling down. Suddenly something changed in the air, all the bulls felt it, and began to look around to see what had caused the change. Several bulls began to walk towards the undergrowth, peering into the darkness, all their senses on high alert to a possible danger.

The older bull had had many experiences in his life, but this odd feeling was new. Something else was in the valley which felt out of place and dangerous. Not snakes, he'd stamp on them if they got too close to him. It was something else, something he couldn't explain, in his mind it was something new and he didn't like it. The other bulls were equally disturbed and were walking around their cows.

Whatever it was out there in the night, he felt it coming close to him, turning fast, as a fear of the unknown took hold of him. He felt something cold touch him, so, so, cold and suddenly he felt a primeval fear, handed down through countless generations of his breed. He uttered a call of danger, one of extreme urgency and began to run towards the end of the valley. Badly spooked the other bulls, weren't waiting around to see what had caused the older bull to run. They followed with the strength of their youth at a great pace, followed by all the cows to get away from this valley. Nothing stopped their rush to get as far as possible from whatever danger was a threat to them amongst these tall hills.

Chapter 44

In the next valley Frank Black was talking to his men about the planned operation, for the next day. They were all looking forward to the promised celebrations at the demise of the Sefton family and all the other police who had opposed their activities.

"All the Seftons are to be shot and everyone who is found with them," Frank stated firmly.

"What about his woman?" Knox asked.

"You can use her and then shoot her, that's a dumb question, William. I want no witnesses, William," he added, then in a very soft voice said to him, "You and I will be the only two people to walk out of this valley, when it's all over."

"What do we do with the bodies?"

"Leave them, the animals can have them."

As a man approached them Frank said, "See what he wants?"

After man had spoken to Knox for a couple of minutes and left Frank asked, :"What did he say?"

"He said the horses have all gone."

"Gone where?"

"He didn't know, the western side of the enclosure was down and he thinks they have gone up into the hills somewhere."

"Fool!!"

"Do you want me to organize men to look for the horses?"

"No, do it in the morning."

"Do you realize tomorrow we will be masters of our world, nothing can stand in our way," Frank said and laughed cheerfully.

As Knox stood up to leave, Frank heard the approaching thunder and asked, "What the hell is that sound?"

Knox who had heard it and had no idea of its source, but felt he had to say something and replied, "Probably an approaching storm."

Suddenly both men turned as one to see death coming under the hooves of a multitude of cattle, running as fast as possible away from an ancient fear.

When the cattle had passed through this valley, not one man was alive, probably better this way than what had been planned for them.

Silence reigned in the valley.

Chapter 45

At the side of the hill facing west, John and Susie Sefton with their son Steve, watched in the moonlight as the cattle stormed past in a massive wave of colours visible in the bright light of the moon. The thunder of their hooves was like iron on the rough ground, being flattened in an instant. It was the most impressive sight and the operation had been months in the planning.

"What spooked the cattle to make them run that fast?" Susie asked.

"I don't know," John replied

"Red told me that this matter was well in hand, he had a friend who would help him, when the time came and the cattle needed to be spooked," Steve explained.

"Do I get the feeling Steve, that you don't want to say exactly what caused the cattle to be spooked?" His father enquired carefully.

"You're correct Dad."

"Why?"

"Some knowledge you don't need to have in your life."

"Isn't that my choice, Steve?"

"No. In this instant, the choice is mine to make and I've made it. The matter is now closed."

"That's what I'd expect from our son!" Susie said, laughing, then continued, "Is it over John, will we be free to live without being afraid of being killed?"

"Susie, there'll be a cleaning up in the city, and I expect we'll be able to leave here soon, but not just yet."

"Do you want the security men to remain here too?" Steve asked.

"I think so Steve, until the core of that group has been laid to rest."

"When will we know?" Steve enquired.

"Tomorrow a message will be sent to the city to tell my men of the death of Frank Black and William Knox. My men will begin arresting the people in Frank's building. No exceptions."

"Why can't Mother go down to my slab hut, while you fix up your end of your business?" Steve commented.

"I believe she'll be more comfortable here."

Susie had listened to her husband and her son talk, without asking her opinion. She was slightly irritated at their lack of manners, talking as if she had not been present. She had been accustomed to making her own decisions and this was one of them. She spoke firmly, "If you two are quite finished?"

John looked surprised and said, "I think so dear."

"Don't dear me John! I've decided to go down to Steve's hut. I'm told it has three rooms attached and Roy is living in it. We'll make a call to Bob Pringle to come with several drays to move our equipment to the hut. Do either of you have anything to say to my plan?"

Wisely both John and his son kept all thoughts to themselves on this matter,

"And the security men?" Steve enquired.

"They'll come too." His father replied.

"There will be someone who'll take your place in the hut when you leave it. He'll have his own bits and pieces. When you leave he'll move in." Steve told his Mother.

"Who is it?" His father asked.

"No one you know Dad, nor does he have anything to do with your problems, just a man who wants to live in seclusion. This is a lovely place to live."

"So you're not telling me?"

"No Dad, you don't need to know him"

John Sefton, who had been accustomed to getting obedience from Steve, suddenly discovered the boy had a mind of his own and could easily sidestep his father, on any issue which suited him. Times were changing!

Chapter 46

The next day Bill, Ian and Rex left their hill and moved down to the valley where the main camp was situated beside water. They were joined by Ken, Jamie and Steve.

"We're looking for any evidence that anything has survived the trashing of the camp by thousands of hooves," they explained.

They rode into a valley, stinking of broken bodies, with bones and body parts scattered everywhere.

"This isn't a good place for horses, can't we do the job on foot?" Rex said.

"I agree with you Rex, we have more chance of finding papers on the ground, than on our horses," Steve replied.

They led their mounts to the opening of the valley behind the bloody field, leaving them eating green grass, looking content.

It took a while to find Frank Black's camp and Steve was able to retrieve his bundle of papers. They were badly damaged with blood and gore splattered through them.

"Cleaned up, you might be able to get some information out of them?" Bill commented.

Rex picked up some money he found scattered on the ground. Bill recognised a necklace which belonged to the girl who worked in the tea tent at Hill Top. He picked it up and would clean it up, before returning it to her. Ian recognised other things which he knew came from Hill Top. Once this search began, they found a lot of things that could be returned to their owners.

"At this rate we'll need a dray or two to take this stuff back to Hill Top," Bill commented.

Steve found enough evidence to create a number of trials in court, and possible work for the hangman.

"Go up through the ranges, following the cattle tracks. You ought to find Harry, Nick, Tony and Allan somewhere up there, or just out in the open country," Steve told Rex after he had completed the job.

He pointed up the valley. Rex had no desire to stay in that place any longer than he was required to. Bill and Ian not in earshot and seeing Rex's expression and guessing his thoughts said, "Go, I'll explain to Bill and Ian that you've gone to help divide the cattle."

Rex already had his swag and some rations and kept his horse at a steady pace to get out of the death valley, and back to good clean grass.

Rex enjoyed the ride up the ranges because the cattle had squashed everything in their rush to escape their nightmare, including all the green grass now churned up in the mud. The river was low enough to be used by the cattle as a path too. Not all the animals had made the journey free of trouble as he discovered, making notes of a couple of dead cows. It looked as if they had fallen and broken a leg, the others had simply charged over the top of them. None would have survived this wave of cattle. Further up the ranges the great wave had stopped its mad rush, settling down to a walking pace, but still with that sense of urgency to escape whatever it felt might be lurking behind in the shadows.

Rex saw no one else on his ride and the cattle were some hours ahead of him. He made camp in the early twilight and enjoyed the peace and quiet after the last couple of days of frantic activity. Leaving again at first light, he rode up between high hills and eventually found the place where the herd had been turned to leave the ranges. As he had seen earlier the wave had resisted for a time, and the ground was really churned up into clumps of mud. Rex followed the tracks down the long valley and at last rode out into open country. This was where Red had organised large yards and a race to divide the cattle for their various owners to claim their stock.

It was a magnificent sight. Riding around the cattle he eventually found the camp on the other side of a deep gully. He rode down the side of the gully for perhaps a mile before finding an animal track to cross it. The job of dividing the stock wasn't an easy one, with horses and their riders moving rapidly this way and that way in an instant. There was also language of a particular type, open to use, the stockmen shouting at the top of their voices to anyone in the yards or nearby trying to move the stock, who usually wanted to go their own way.

Slowly the various branded cattle were being separated and their owners began to take them to other areas, before the long trip back to their land in the south. None of the men wanted to leave until the job was completed and everyone had their own stock.

"You saved the horses, they're now yours to do as you like with them, take them away or turn them loose," Rex had been told before he left the hill in the ranges.

In the camp he saw a man from Sunny Flat who didn't seem to be engaged in the cattle work, just sitting in front of the fire.

"Do you want a job Alec?" Rex said as he walked across to him.

"What kind of a job do you have in mind?"

"I've a herd of horses which need to be taken back to Sunny Flat."

"We've never been friends Rex, why are you asking me to do this job?"

"You're right, we've never been friends, but I know my horses will be safe with you. These horses haven't been treated properly recently, they need careful handling. You are the best man for the job."

"Where do I take the horses to in Sunny Flat?"

"To my father," Adding with a laugh, "He doesn't know they are coming. What's your fee for the job?"

"How many horses are in the herd?"

"Fifty or sixty."

"A choice of two horses would be fair considering the distance involved."

"Okay, that sounds satisfactory."

They shook hands on the deal and Alec asked for directions to find the horses and left.

In the evening Tony and Allan arrived at the camp, tired and satisfied with their day's work.

"Have you seen Alec Brick?" Tony asked Rex.

"Yes, I needed a man to take a few horses back to Sunny Flat. I've employed Alec to do the job. He's very good with horses."

"Rex, we have a big job to do here and need all the help we can get. You send a man away for a couple of horses," Tony said, bristling immediately.

"Not exactly a couple of horses, Tony, but at last count between fifty and sixty," Rex replied in a calming voice.

"What?"

"You heard me."

"How did you come by that number of horses?"

"Later after the meal I'll tell you. I'll take Alec's place for a day or so. What have you done today?"

"We've divided up Red's cattle and Kevin took them back to him this afternoon. The other men have taken cattle out of the herd, but keeping them from wandering away is a problem," Allan replied.

"And your cattle?"

"We've them penned up in the next valley and will divide them when we get home."

"Several of the other owners are doing it the same way, we've come to enjoy each other's company. This will help to make a better community back home," Tony added.

"We want to know what spooked the cattle so much that they were still moving at a steady pace when we turned them out of the ranges?" Allan enquired.

"I don't really know what it was that spooked them so badly, but it was something which created a mortal fear in them."

"Who or what brought it to the valley?" Tony asked.

"I heard it was from the distant past, something belonging to an ancient time which was held in mortal fear by other animals. I don't know nor do I want to know Tony," Rex replied, clearly uncomfortable.

His explanation wasn't enough to satisfy his friends who wanted more details, after all they had played a significant part in this operation. They understood he was a policeman and couldn't reveal much about what had led to the conclusion in the ranges.

"Rex please can you be a bit more open with us?" Tony enquired carefully.

He thought about Tony's request during the meal, as the other men joined the group around the fire. Night had fallen, and a couple of other men were riding around the herds of cattle in their various locations.

Rex began to talk quietly beginning with his rescue of the horses, leading to what he had witnessed. Not a word was spoken as he talked, lost in a world of his memory, totally unaware when other men came to listen to his quiet voice.

These men would relate this story again and again, around campfires and cattle camps until the original story was lost.

ACKNOWLEDGEMENTS

This is my second year of learning to use a computer. The pages don't disappear as often as they used to – only vanishing if I type less than one page.

I'm still typing with one finger, but at a faster rate than I did in the previous books of this series. I have also found an improvement in my spelling and English.

I wish to thank Wendy Morrow for her work in correcting sentences and other errors, before forwarding it to the publisher, Sam Everingham, who is also supportive in his suggestions for a better script. I greatly appreciate his comments.

I also wish to thank Kayla Arkinstall and Huw Moore for coming to my house to put my work on USB drives – something I haven't mastered as yet.

Lastly I would like to thank Ted Lewis for the use of one of his paintings on the front cover of this book.

This trilogy has come to an end. Book number four will be a new story with some of the main characters from the previous books plus new ones.

I'm enjoying the challenge. My troops at the local Police Station have grown up from Kindergarten with computers, whereas I learnt to use a pen which I dipped in the ink well at the Carcoar Public School in 1954. I remember the girl who sat in front of my desk had lovely golden hair in plaits and I got the ruler for dipping the end of her plaits in the blue ink well. I also remember riding a horse to school that year for the whole year. Different times.

I appreciate my troops encouragement in my writing and their offers of help with modern technology. It is most appreciated.

www.ingramcontent.com/pod-product-compliance
Lightning Source LLC
Chambersburg PA
CBHW071150180726
48291CB00007B/2407